THE NEXUS

AND OTHER STORIES

Elise Abram

EMSA
PUBLISHING

ALSO BY ELISE ABRAM

The New Recruit

I Was, Am, Will Be Alice

The Revenant: A YA Paranormal Thriller with Zombies

Phase Shift

Throwaway Child

The Mummy Wore Combat Boots

CONTENTS

Not of this World 7

    Aliens' Waltz 9

    The Arrival V1 17

    The Arrival V3 21

The Future 25

    Hope Floats 27

    Watercolour World 37

    A Morgan by any other Name 39

Ghost Stories 51

    Bubby's Garden 53

    The Earl of Oswald's Revenge 57

The Supernatural 65

    The Circle of Life 67

    At the Mere Thought Of 71

    The Last Supper 75

    Leather Bat 81

    The Nexus 83

NOT OF THIS WORLD

ALIENS' WALTZ

There's an anomaly in the midst of Sheppard Mercant's wheat field. It's an anomaly unlike any other of its kind, though there are others through which parallels may be drawn. Mercant's anomaly forms a perfect square. Inside the square are rings. Inside each ring is a perfect, five-point star. The anomaly extends for metres in any direction. Standing on the cusp of Mercant's field, one is hard-put to see it as different from any other field. But as one nears the centre of the field, tall, lanky stems give way to a clearing. Inside the clearing, the wheat is bent as if steamed.

It's always bent; never broken. If it's authentic.

I'd spent the better part of the morning pacing the pattern, hopping from one ring to another, measuring, photographing, and making notes. I felt energized, and that was bad. It meant there was something wrong with the anomaly. After spending so much time inside it, I should have had a headache. I should have felt dizzy. My camera should have been on the fritz. No, I'd examined enough of these anomalies to know something wasn't right.

I tell Mercant and he can't believe it. He swears he's seen lights hovering in his field. Swears his farm was shut down tight for the night, no one's come or gone for hours. Says he found the anomaly at the crack of dawn. Was up with the roosters. Takes my discovery personal, like it's an accusation. Kicks me off his property like it's my fault he's been hoaxed.

No sooner have I zipped shaving kit into overnight bag than my phone rings. Sheriff Pete calling. Another crop circle reported early this morning.

I arrive at the site still close to dawn. Woven into the canola is a three-dimensional pattern of circles.

Another anomaly.

I set up on the inside border of the largest circle in the arrangement. The display on my camera goes wonky. A good sign.

Stalks are blown out at the nodes. It happens when moisture inside steams and bursts out like popped corn. Another good sign.

Sheriff Pete holds one end of a cloth tape. I take the other and walk the distance to the far side of the anomaly. She's a good size, this one is. Record the length. Record the width. Make note of the weave of the stalks. I'd take a picture but my camera's useless. That's the problem with technology—the more sophisticated it is, the likelier it'll be taken out by even the tiniest of EM fields. What I wouldn't give for a mechanical thirty-five mil. You'd think I'd have learned by now. My theory: is it's genetic. Buried deep in the Y chromosome there's a technology gene.

"What'd ya think, Joey?" Sheriff Pete asks. I correct him mentally; I much prefer Josef.

Hands on hips and suppressing a smile I shake my head. "So far so good, Pete. The farmer still around? What's his name?"

"Corey. Dan Corey."

"I need to speak with Farmer Dan, then."

"Try to show a little respect, will ya, Joey? Farmin' ain't as glamorous as book publishin', I know, but don't belittle him like that when ya see him, eh?"

I wave Sheriff Pete off and concentrate on the anomaly.

Time ticks by. The pounding starts in my right temple. Now I have to decide: is it the usual migraine? Too much sun through too little hair? Something else?

Migraine or sun would be bad. Means Farmer Dan's been hoaxed, too.

Something else, on the other hand...

Something else would be out of this world.

Pun intended.

Sheriff Pete returns, Farmer Dan quick on his heels.

Farmer Dan's unaware of human presence in his field. He throws in sightings of low, hovering lights three days running, for good measure.

Back at Sheriff Pete's office, Officer Sweaty Pits brings in a kid in cuffs.

"For God's sakes, Rocky! What the hell do ya think you're doin'?" Sheriff Pete hollers. "That's Matt Donohue's boy ya got there. Let him go."

"Caught him in Flannigan's field, boss," Officer Sweaty Pits says. "Playin' with this." He drops a two-by-four, two fiberglass measuring tapes, and a blueprint traced onto graph paper onto Sheriff Pete's desk. "At least three others got away."

While Sheriff Pete tries to convince Officer Sweaty Pits to release his prisoner, I examine the two-by-four. Rough rope ties around either end to make a harness. Heavy rope. One foot at rest on the two-by-four flattens the growth while the other balances on the ground. A second man holds the tape at the centre of the circle. Acts like a human compass.

I exchange the rope for the blueprint. Nice. Symmetrical. Like in Mercant's field.

Symmetry's overrated.

Farmer Dan's was different. Asymmetrical, but balanced.

Officer Sweaty Pits thrusts his considerable nose at me. "What's this guy doin' here?"

"This here's Joey Schliemann. He's here to investigate the crop circles."

I wince. I much prefer "anomaly". It's the subtle difference between serious and sensational.

"Hey, I've seen you before, man," Donohue Junior chimes in. "On TV. Dude! You're the documentary dude. That show! What's it called?"

"'Pseudo, Not Science'," I offer. Regrettably, one of my most lucrative and bothersome endeavors.

"You rock, dude!" Uncuffed at this point, he leaps out of his chair and offers me a knuckled fist. I respond in kind. He turns it into a secret handshake. My fingers go limp but maintain just enough body to play along.

"This is the *man!*" Donohue Junior tells Sheriff Pete and Officer Sweaty Pits as he sits. "His show? Gave me the idea."

I'm not sure whether to be proud or embarrassed at the revelation.

"Okay, Warren, let's start at the beginning, eh?" Sheriff Pete asks.

"I'm arrestin' him for vandalism, boss."

"Now hold on a second there, Rocky. Warren's our local golden boy. He's just graduated from university down there in Waterloo. Why'd a boy who studied Math want to go ahead and vandalize anythin' for?"

"Vandalism," Golden Boy snorts. This was getting good.

"Caught 'em packin' up after they'd vandalized Flannigan's field. He and his buddies. Puttin' their crop circles all over it."

"One man's vandalism is another man's art."

"Hush, Warren, okay? Now, if what Rocky's sayin' is true, ya could be in a whole lot of trouble here."

"If I may?" I ask, jumping in on my own accord. "*You're* the one who's been making the anomalies in the fields?"

Hushed, Golden Boy nods.

"For God's Sakes, Warren. Art Flannigan's your great uncle. Why'd ya wanna go destroyin' his wheat crop like that?"

"Come on, Petey," Golden Boy whines. Sheriff Pete clears his throat and looks uncomfortable at Golden Boy's familiarity. "You know as well as I do that no one ever gets out unless they do something to get noticed."

"And ya think destruction of property's the way to do it?"

Golden Boy hitches a thumb in my direction. "Got *him* here didn't it?"

My shoulders shrug; lips form a thin smile.

"Somehow I don't think Kingston Pen is what ya had in mind for gettin' out," says Sheriff Pete.

"You claim to have made *all* of the crop circles?" I ask Golden Boy.

"Mercant's. And Flannigan's. Can I have your autograph?"

"Not Corey's?"

"*Daniel* Corey? He's got one too? No *way*, man!"

"Have you done others?"

"Now hold on a second there, Joey," Sheriff Pete interrupts. "Ya don't have to answer that, Warren. Not if it's goin' to incriminate ya."

"I'll mention you by name in my next book."

"Three others." Golden Boy lists them off.

"You got a map handy?" I ask Sheriff Pete.

A map depicting each anomaly hangs on the wall behind Sheriff Pete's desk. He points it out.

"A marker?"

Sheriff Pete finds one in a coffee mug on his desk. Hands it to me. I toss it at Golden Boy.

"Show me which ones are yours. Cross them off. Every one."

Golden Boy looks at me apprehensive.

"With impunity," I say.

Golden Boy looks at Sheriff Pete apprehensive.

Sheriff Pete nods.

Golden Boy goes to the map and exes out almost half. What remains forms an obvious north-north-east by south-south-west pattern.

Stake out time. I've got a fifty-fifty chance. I toss a coin. North by north-east it is.

Third day on my roost on the hill on the Crane farm. Managed to convince Farmer Crane's wife not to bring me any more coffee after the first few hours of the first day. Best

14

if I'm left alone. Watch says it's well past midnight. Time to pack it in. Camera goes first. Still not mechanical. Hicksville, Ontario. Would think you'd have a hard time finding digital instead.

I'm zipping up my camera bag when something catches my eye. A light. Hovering. In and around the wheat stalks. Now two. Soon joined by a third. Flitting back and forth in scrutiny.

The lights disappear. Abruptly. All at once. Then, a bright flash. Lightning, I might believe, but then there they stand. Two figures. Tall. Draped in incandescent oyster they assume a face-to-face stance, arms forming a loose square. At once, they begin to sway to silent music.

Slowly move, quick box step, twirling round, open, turn. One-two-three, two-two-three. Shoulders rise. Fall again. Moving on a single plane, tall and completely poised. Triangular faces showcase ovular eyes. Smoky and luminous in celestial moonlight. Fabric of dress gowns shine, twinkling in the night. One-two-three, two-two-three, weightlessly promenade. Steam buoys from wheat stalks forming nebulous mist. Feet barely skim farmland in a spiraling glide.

Floating. Hovering. Refined. Gently bending wheat stalks in their wake.

A uniform stop, audible pause in inaudible music. They disappear. Reappear. Relocate. Chests rise and fall in breath. Then begin again.

Up forward down, up forward down...

Round and round. Suspended above the crop. Lighter than air. In and about the existing circle.

Faster and faster. Ever graceful, elastic, elegant, then stop.

They pause, each holding the other, arms square. Shoulders rise and fall in breath on a single plain.

Lights flash from overhead. Multicoloured. Illuminating the wheat field. Visual applause from the audience overhead. Discernable silence joins the existing auditory lapse.

A bright flash and I'm alone amongst the wheat stalks. In the dark.

Daybreak irradiates the dawn; spotlights the anomaly in the field. One large circle dotted with seven smaller circles around its perimeter. Cookie-cut outs. Asymmetrical footprints left behind by the aliens as they danced their waltz bathed in moonlight's silvery illume.

THE ARRIVAL V1

They came to tell the world, just because they could. They came to tell us they were alive; they came to help us; they came to share with us. They came, and then they left. And the future of the world was changed forever.

My name is Jones, and I'm an anthropologist. Please, don't confuse me with that other Jones: I study the culture of living societies; he relished in the cultural objects of dead ones. I've been pretty much all over this world and it's true what they say: the more things change, the more they stay the same. With each and every passing year, I realize that people are people are people. We all cherish our families, celebrate our triumphs, and mourn our losses; we all strive for greatness and wallow in the self-pity of defeat; we all are born, live, breathe, and bleed, and we all die. People are people are people. The one thing we have not yet learned to do is to respect other people while they are being...well...people.

In the whole history of the world, people have fought. People have killed other people over love, over hate, over religion, over a principle, no matter how pointless. Why, in my lifetime alone, I've witnessed the Viet Nam War, the Gulf War, as well as countless other skirmishes in Bosnia and the Middle East. People never learn. And war's just the tip of the iceberg. Let us not forget about what we're doing to our planet—it's a wonder we've even come this far; it's a wonder they stuck around for as long as they did.

And yet, they did. Five years, by their account, playing Hide and Go Seek with the moon and our Mars probes until, one day, they entered our atmosphere and made their presence known; I swear it was a scene right out of *Independence Day*. We all saw it on the news. Saw it as it happened, right on CP24, in between reports of anti-terrorist laws and the latest suicide bombing. The ship, looming large as it cast its shadow over The White House, the people on the ground, craning their necks to get a good look, drawn as insects to a light after dark, hands raised in mock-salute to shield their eyes from the sun's glare on its black-silver hull.

We watched as reports came of beings shuttling to Earth to meet with world leaders. We listened as people claimed sightings around the globe. We shuddered at the reported abductions, real or imagined, denied by the visitors. We studied police-artist drawings dictated by eyewitnesses. And through it all, we were reminded of that one axiom that traversed even hundreds of light years, ringing true throughout the galaxy: people are people are people. We all have a head, eyes, nose, ears, a single mouth. We all have four limbs, arms with hands, and legs with feet. We all have a brain with which we weigh reason and possibility and pass judgment.

The American President urged the American public not to panic: "They chose America for first contact," he boasted. "They chose Freedom. They chose Democracy." They chose a leader with a good speechwriter.

The Canadian Prime Minister urged the rest of us not to panic: "Our friends and allies to the south," he enunciated, "will make first contact. Our continental brethren will extend the olive branch in our stead." Once more, the Canadian public chided him for not rushing to Washington to be in the middle of the action, for not being more...American.

They came. They met with the President of the United States, still, after all the terror and devastation, the leader of the most powerful nation in the world. They saw the flags and the wreckage of Ground Zero; they marveled at the technology and the tainted air; they scoffed at the promises and Band-Aid fixes we profess to procure.

And in the end, there was silence. There was no fanfare to welcome us in alliance; no cure to our ills; no key to unlock the solution to the shortcomings of the human race. Only silence. Silence as they turned; silence as they closed the shuttle door; silence as they returned to the mothership; silence as the behemoth slipped from the sunshine, through the atmosphere, and from the solar system.

Yes, in the end, they had come to tell the world they were out there, and the future of the world was changed forever. They had come from a world without war, without famine, without disease, without pollution. They had come to our world to tell us how they did it and they left in disgust. They had come to tell us they were alive, and left as co-conspirators in the composition our death warrant.

THE ARRIVAL V3

NORAD first picked it up on the radar when it dropped into orbit, a huge blip the size of a football field. Within seven minutes, sixteen F-18 fighter jets arrived on the scene to escort the black-silver disk to its destination: the airspace over The White House. For miles, people were frozen in their tracks as deer held by oncoming headlights at the scene, ripped from *Independence Day* celluloid. An audible gasp sounded from the crowd as a panel slid open in the otherwise unbroken hull, and a cigar-shaped shuttle emerged into the daylight—its movement buoyant and fluid at once—and landed on the manicured lawn of 1600 Pennsylvania Avenue. Once more, a panel slid open, two beings emerged, and in typical "take me to your leader" fashion, climbed the stairs of The White House, conversed with the guard on watch, and entered the building.

Voiced over a shaky cell phone video representation of the event, Tom Brokaw boomed: "And now, after five years of covert observation, you can finally see the small shuttle landing...and the door opening...and...yes...there they are: the aliens.

"We take you live now to Connie Chung, stationed just outside The White House Gates. Connie?" The camera remained on Tom for brief seconds before dissolving to split-screen, revealing Connie, perfectly made-up and neatly coiffed in her black and white, hound's-tooth-checked, Chanel suit.

"Tom? Are you there, Tom?"

"Connie?" he responded, "Connie, can you tell us what the scene was like on The White House steps earlier this hour as the visitors arrived?"

"Tom?" She tapped her earpiece with her index finger, then addressed the cameraman: "Am I on? Am I...Tom?"

"It seems..."

"I can't...I can't hear him...Tom?"

"We seem to be having a technical difficulty," Tom diagnosed as the split-screen dissolved back to a full-screen close-up of him alone. "We'll work on it and get back to Connie who will describe the scene earlier this hour as fraught with curiosity and expectation."

The presidential aides expressed quieted concern when the aliens requested tours of Ground Zero, water treatment plants, and homeless shelters. Parliament Hill confirmed they had nothing to hide when the aliens asked to visit their nuclear power plant reactors. The democratic world held its breath as the president actively carried out damage control, defending his actions in his newfound War on Terrorism, collectively cringing with each new incident of suicide bombing as it was publicized.

The president addressed the nation. In a carefully scripted speech, he urged the American public not to panic: "They chose America for first contact," he boasted. "They chose Freedom. They chose Democracy."

In Canada, the Prime Minister followed suit: "Our friends and allies to the south," he enunciated, "will make first contact. Our continental brethren will extend the olive branch in our stead." Rather than extol him for waiting for an invitation to the meet and greet—which was the Canadian thing to do—the Canadian public chastised him for not being more American and storming The White House to demand a face-to-face meeting.

An emergency gathering of the world's leaders was called. The aliens asked each and every one of them the most simply phrased question in the world and the most difficult to answer: "Why?

"On our world, we do not kill each other to benefit ourselves. We do not hoard food. We have eradicated disease. We do not destroy the very air we breathe in the name of technology and convenience.

"Why has an intelligent race, such as yourselves, not learned from its mistakes?"

A cacophony of voices materialized. Individual voices were lost as the din rose. Some leaders yelled in defense of their countries' actions. Others urged for a worldwide summit to discuss solutions to the problem. In the ensuing chaos, the beings slipped out unnoticed, and returned, first to their shuttle, and then to their ship.

At once, the prattle was broken by a gavel pounding on a table; a loud, booming noise that echoed throughout the theatre, followed by silence.

"Hey," a single voice said, interrupting the newly settled silence, "where did they go?"

They left—first the atmosphere, and then the solar system, never to return, sealing the fate of the world forever.

THE FUTURE

HO?E FLOATS

I climbed out from the rubble to feel the sunshine on my face for the first time in a while, though I don't remember how long. I know how to keep time, that's not the problem. It's just that these days, we tend to rely on the maws and paws to keep track for us. It's their responsibility to tell us when we've had too much of anything. Too much sleep. Too much fun. As if I'm not old enough to figure that out on my own. "I swear, if I didn't tell you when it was time to pee, you'd probably wet yourself. Repeatedly," Mawbea is fond of saying. Like more happened on that day than the end of The Before, like every prepubescent in the world was suddenly struck with a case of The Dumbs.

If I was so dumb, how did I find my way to the surface? I'd heard from some of the older sibs there was a way out from under the city. I'd kept my plan a secret for days, watching the maws as they went about their business. I was quiet enough so's they hardly noticed I was there when they shared stories of the battle scars they'd picked up on their last quest to the surface.

Over the weeks I'd watched them, studied them, until I'd come up with a quest of my own: to bring back something to help ease the food shortage. "Leave the mawin' to the maws and the pawin' to the paws," Mawbea would say, but that didn't make much sense. If I could do something better than the maws—or even the paws, for that matter—why shouldn't I be able to do it? The maws and paws were always coming up with sayings like that that never made much sense to me. One day, when I got angry at her and refused to eat my food for no other reason than because she'd prepared it, Mawbea told me I was being silly, that I had to eat my food when I could because there wouldn't always be food in The Pantry to put on my plate. She told me I was cutting off my nose to spite my face. I wanted her to know I was, in fact, quite the opposite of silly, so I said, "Aw, Mawbea, you know as well as I do that cutting off my nose would more spoil than spite my face." Mawbea stared at me for a long moment, then pushed my plate closer to my body. "Eat, child," she said, worriedly. "Protein's good for the brain." She reached across the table for my fork, fished around in my bowl, stabbed a piece of whatever meat it was in the stew that evening, and held it out for me. I took it from her and slid the grey chunk from the fork into my mouth. "Good boy," she said as my teeth wrestled with the meat. "Enough silliness," and she left the table to scavenge The Pantry's store for the fixings for our next meal.

I waited until Mawellen went for her afternoon nap, and Mawbea got busy in the kitchen stretching out what was left in The Pantry to feed us all so the littlesibs wouldn't have to cry themselves to sleep hungry before sneaking out.

Broken concrete is heavy. I brought knit gloves for my hands and wore long pants and high boots to protect myself from the rusty bars poking from the wreckage, like broken bones through pale flesh. The older sibs called the rusty bars

Snakes because, like a snake, one bite could kill you. One of the sibs, a pudgy, grey boy with a gruff voice and chronic case of volcano-face said he'd heard of someone from The Before who stepped on a rusty nail and nearly died when the poison from the bite got into his blood, in spite of the fact it was The Before, when there was medicine to take care of things like that. Tent-ass, it was called. The boys laughed till they were blue in the face, even the grey boy, because he'd said "ass". When they calmed down, another sib, a boy with smoky skin and knotted, mud-coloured hair, pointed out that it had been because of a nail, not a Snake. The Concrete Snakes, the grey sib explained, were also made of old rusty metal, and it didn't matter if one was a nail and one was a Snake. When you were bit, you were bit, and we had to be extra careful we weren't bit, because of Tent-ass. Once again, the sibs cracked up. I did too, a bit. The grey sib was brave. The maws promised that if I ever swore, one of them would wash my mouth out with soap. This threat worked on two levels. First, none of the sibs I knew would ever actively seek out an opportunity to eat soap, no matter how hungry. Second, like everything else, soap was in short supply since after The Before and we would shame to waste a supply as dear as soap for something as crass as swearing. At least, that was how Mawellen had explained it.

The sun was warm on my face, warm like when I stood in front of the stove and the wood burned and crackled inside. The air smelled of sunshine and possibility, like anything could happen, like I could do anything I'd set my mind to, like the eternal springs of hope, or something Mawbea used to say like that. I squatted in a patch of grass at the side of the rubble, looking for whatever surface life I could see. Squirrel, if I was lucky. Rat was meatier. If I was really lucky,

I might net myself a raccoon, a big, fat, maw raccoon, and all her babies. Mawellen told us a story once, about when she was younger, in The Before, when families lived in brick and wood houses on the surface in groups with only one maw, one paw, and one or two sibs. Before, the sibs in each family were Related, which meant they shared the same blood, and half of each sib's blood came from their maw and half from their paw. Anyway, Mawellen's family had this thing called a Fridge, a large box that ran on Energy and kept food cold. They had this thing called Cake for a meal called Dessert, but most of the Cake had been left over, so Mawellen's maw put the Cake in the Fridge and her whole family forgot about it until it had turned blue and green, and they threw it out. Mawellen's whole family were woken that night by this big fat maw raccoon that had knocked the trash bin over and pulled the Cake out. By the time they were able to reach a window, the maw raccoon and her babies were already feeding on the Cake.

Mawellen had told us the story to demonstrate how smart and resourceful raccoons were and that we shouldn't underestimate them. I thought it proved the exact opposite—why would anyone, human or otherwise, want to eat anything that had grown blue-green moss on it?

Though many of us had never had Cake before, we had heard stories from the maws and paws about what it was and how it had tasted, making it hard for some of the littlesibs to get to sleep that night. Sibsimon couldn't get past the thought of sweet, pillowy Cake covered in creamy icing. He complained his mouth was watering so, he might drown if he fell asleep. Sibtom grew angrier each time he thought of how Mawellen lectured us if we'd neglected even a single morsel, a single crumb of food on our plates, and here, her family let a near-whole, luscious, feathery, elusive Cake go to waste.

Cake. I vowed if I could find some, I'd bring that back, too. All the maws and paws, and all the sibs would hail me as the bravest, smartest sib who ever lived. A hero, by Mawlou's definition, is a man who does what he can. Dinner *and* Dessert. Since I was already on the surface, I would do what I could.

I heard a squeaky warble overhead, and a small, white bird soared to a tree in the distance. Though not what I had hoped for, nevertheless, a bird that size might yield enough meat for Fancy Rice and Beans or Pot Pie. Careful to avoid the Snakes hiding in and amongst the fallen concrete, I searched to find some two or three pieces that would fit in the palm of my hand, which I loaded into my satchel before following the bird to the tree.

The bird sat in the foliage of the low tree branch, cooing and preening. The first chunk of concrete fell short, missing the branch and bird entirely. The second piece flew through the leaves with a rustle and a crack. The bird took off. I made sure I was alone before I swore.

I fell to the grass to sulk, pulling out tall green blades by the handfuls. Then something moved in the distance. I looked up to see bright white, waving wings. The wings flapped slowly up and down as the butterfly relaxed on the tall grass, then lifted up once more and fluttered away as if riding on the wind. I got up and followed it, across the field and up a hill until it rested on the branch of an almond tree. Slowly, so as not to scare it off, I neared the butterfly and cupped it in my hand. I took the box I'd packed into my satchel, nudged the butterfly into it and sealed the box with the lid. I thought of the look on Sibrachel's face when she'd open the box and the butterfly would fly out. She'd giggle to herself, blush, and kiss me on the cheek. Though I'd try hard not to blush myself, I wouldn't be able to help it. Then she'd tell me how cute I was. I liked Sibrachel…a lot. I thought of her pink, round face and bottle green eyes as I listened to the scritch-scratch of the butterfly's wings against the lid of the box. I snapped a few branches off the almond tree, blossoms in full bloom, the colour of Sibrachel's cheeks, for some of the maws, then bent to arrange them in my satchel.

The cooing began again as the white bird flew overhead in the direction of its last roost. I raced back across the field to the tree. The bird walked, herky-jerky across the branch, looking first this way, then that, as if making sure the coast was clear. Slowly, I found the last hunk of concrete in my satchel. Taking a moment to aim, I tossed it at the bird and hit it square on. The cooing stopped. The bird fell. It lay, white, red, and unmoving in the grass under the shade of the tree.

I neared at a snail's pace, unsure of what had just happened. "Get up, bird," I said. I nudged it with the tip of my boot toe, but it didn't listen. "Up, bird!" I told it, moving it an inch or two when I nudged it again. "Fly!" Nothing happened. Ignoring the blood seeping from the gash on its chest, I picked it up, smoothed its feathers, and tossed it into the air. "I said, 'Fly!'" It travelled a few feet under my power then plummeted to the ground with a thud. I stared at it a long time where it landed, willing it to coo once more, but it wouldn't; it was dead.

I wanted to cry; it was my first kill. Ever. I wanted to laugh; I was a provider, a Paw-In-The-Making. I wanted to preen in front of all the maws and paws, but especially in front of Sibrachel. I withdrew an old scarf from my satchel, wrapped the bird in it, and placed it gently back in the satchel. I sat there, I don't know exactly for how long, surrounded by the grass, greener than green, thinking about the dead bird in my satchel, the snow white butterfly in the box, Sibrachel, and the cheek-pink almond blossom sprigs, not knowing how to feel. I'd survived the surface. I was a Hunter. I was a Killer. I would win Sibrachel's heart, but I had broken my own. If this was how it felt to be a paw, I wanted nothing of it.

The sun travelled across the sky. The blue behind the clouds grew dark. The silver sliver of the new moon shone beside the setting sun. Time to go home. I backtracked across the field to the concrete pile, dodging Snakes and falling only once before I'd found the entrance to the underground.

When I'd reached home, Mawlou was sick with worry and Mawbea said, "I was absolutely beside myself." I thought to ask how she could be beside herself unless she was twins and even then...Maybe if she were standing beside her own reflection in a mirror, but I was wallowing too deep in self-pity to say.

Mawlou dried her eyes on her shirtsleeve and helped me off with my satchel. She opened it and pulled out the boughs of almond blossom. "I brought you a present," I told her. "You can have one, too," I told Mawbea. "The other's for Mawellen." I sat at the wooden kitchen table and propped my head on my hands. She took out the butterfly box. "Don't open it!" I called. The chair shot out from under me with a clatter as I reached for the box, but it was too late.

The butterfly hovered overhead, flapping its wings, floating back and forth in the quiet air. I followed it across the room, reaching for it each time it dropped near. It eventually flew over the sink and was sucked into the air duct. "No!" I called, but it was too late. I felt my whole body droop. Mawbea put an arm around my shoulders and whispered that it'd be all right.

"You don't understand," I said, tearing from her grasp. "That was Sibrachel's." But I think they might have understood, at least a little. They gave each other a sideways glance and smiled. "It's not funny," I told them.

"We're not laughing, child," Mawbea said. "We understand. And so will Sibrachel."

"She won't," I said, my voice catching like when the littlesibs tried to stop crying.

"Forget about Sibrachel's affections for now, little one," Mawlou said. "There's still plenty of time for that." If she could say that, she didn't really understand much after all. I had gone on my first hunt. I was a paw, now. I had to think about things like Sibrachel and our future. "Let me fix you some Thin Soup," she said.

"I don't want Thin Soup," I said, angrily. I dumped the rest of my satchel on the kitchen table. The blood-stained scarf that held the bird fell out.

"What is this?" Mawlou asked.

Mawbea gasped. "Is that blood?"

I unwrapped the bird. It lay on the table. It didn't move. It didn't sing. Its black eyes stared off, unseeing into the distance.

"Is that a dove, Lou?" Mawbea said, quietly.

"I think so, Bea." They seemed upset. Both pulled a chair from the table and sat.

"My love," Mawbea said once she'd taken a moment to compose herself. "It is all well and good to have hope, but hope is a ghost."

"And it must remain so," Mawlou added.

"Now," Mawlou said, "do you think we could do anything with this bird, Bea?"

"Absolutely, Lou." Then to me, she asked, "What's your preference, child?"

I thought of Sibrachel's butterfly, back on the surface by now, floating in the night air under the thin crescent moon. "I had hoped for Fancy Rice and Beans," I said with a sniffle.

"Fancy Rice and Beans it is," Mawbea said.

WATERCOLOUR WORLD

Without my glasses, the world is a wet watercolour, a portrait taken with uneven hand. Lying in my bed, I believe I can almost see the light which will take me into its warm embrace and put an end to my pain. I put my glasses on and the world comes clear, my saviour light nothing more than the pinprick of a street lamp whose glare seeps between the slats of the window blind.

I am alone.

A MORGAN BY ANY OTHER NAME

"**F**reak!" she screamed, baring her claw-like nails as she lunged at me.

I stared dumbly, trying to figure out what had happened, my hands raised in defence. Long strands of auburn hair hung between my fingers, papery layer of skin still clinging to the roots. The Morgans suffered chronic Alopecia, an unfortunate replication error that hadn't been caught until after they'd been born. But that wasn't why we were pitted against each other in mortal combat in the school cafeteria. I had nothing against the Morgans or the Heathers or the Julias or any other model in my cohort or any other cohort, for that matter. Being naturally conceived, the Morgans and the Heathers and the Julias had something against me. And all others of my kind.

Rachel, the Morgan-model in question, shrieked at the sight of her extensions cat's cradled between my fingers. "I'll kill you!" A drop of blood trickled down her hairline. She blinked it away and advanced on me.

"I'm sorry, Morgan, I..." I gasped when I realized what I'd said. I was in shock. I was confused. I combed the hair from between my fingers. Some of it fell to the ground, resembling corn silk where it lay. The rest of it clung to my fingers, sticky and fine as cobweb threads.

A collective gasp rose from the gathering crowd. To refer to them, any of them, by their model name was derogatory. I hadn't meant to insult her, to add fuel to the flame.

"*What* did you call me?" She froze, tableau-fashion, blood-red fingernails at the ready.

"I apologized, *Rachel*," I said in a lame attempt at a cover-up. I regretted that her model had slipped out, but there was no convincing Rachel it had been an unintentional faux pas.

"Oh, you are *so* dead," she said calmly and reached for my face.

A hand extended from the sea of students to grab her wrist. The students parted to let Mr. Marsden enter the circle. A First-Gen Michael, Mr. Marsden was perfect. His cohort suffered from acute near-sightedness, but it was nothing a little Lasik couldn't correct. His dreamy violet-blues were none the worse for it. "My office." He dropped Rachel's arm. It slapped her jeans-clad thigh with a thud. "Now!"

A narrow pathway cleared to let him through with a loud "Ooooh," the taunt of impending doom.

All eyes were on me. I'd broken the one, most important rule of high school survival: never call attention to the Clones. It was okay to ignore them, to befriend them, even to date them, but never, ever, call attention to the circumstance of their birth. But that wasn't why I was being marched to Marsden's office. I was in my predicament because of the double-standard. There was no similar taboo governing the behaviour of the Clones who relished calling attention to those of natural birth. Because they considered natural birth to be unclean, they had no desire to befriend us or date us—if only they'd chosen to ignore us.

Marsden sat behind his desk, steepling his fingertips under his chin. "What seems to be the problem here?" he asked. "Lina?" he said, batting his violet-blues at me.

"Oh, sure. Take her side," Rachel said, pouting.

"Rachel, please." He smiled at me. "Lina?"

"I don't know," I said.

"How about you, Rachel, do you know?"

Rachel had started the fight, insulting my parents, implying my parents had been rabid when I was conceived and that I was feral as a result, more animal than human. Okay, so I'd been the first to lay hands on her, but she'd deserved it.

To my surprise, Rachel shook her head. "Nope," she said.

"This wouldn't have anything to do with Birthright now, would it?" Birthright was the latest human rights group to earn media exposure these days. Their Toronto Branch had made the news recently for a peaceful protest that had turned quite violent. Rather than preach equality for all people, Birthright urged Clones to segregate themselves from Natural Borns to rise above their baser, animal instincts.

Both Rachel and I shook our heads. This had everything to do with Birthright on her end and everything to do with self-preservation on mine.

Marsden frowned. "Well, we can't have students facing off against each other in the cafeteria for no reason." He sighed. "I'm afraid you leave me no choice. Your consequence is for the two of you to spend time together. In classes you share and in-between, you'll be joined at the hip, so to speak."

"You can't do that," Rachel whined.

"It's already done."

"Mr. Marsden?" Rachel said, voice sweet as honey. "How is that a punishment for Lina? I mean, isn't hanging with me and my friends more of an opportunity for Lina and those of her kind?"

"It's a consequence, Rachel. You decide whether to make it a punishment or an opportunity." We both stood to leave, equally horrified at our assigned 'consequence'. "Oh, and you may not hang out with your friends for the duration. As far as the two of you are concerned, you are each other's 'kind', the only two like you in the world."

"How long?" I said, hoarsely.

"Twenty-four hours."

"What?" Rachel cried.

"Okay, forty-eight."

"Twenty-four would be acceptable, I guess," Rachel said.

Marsden chuckled. "Glad to hear it," he said.

The next morning, I waited for Rachel in the school's foyer. She air-kissed a Carol on her way in. She had the same overbite as all of the Carols in her cohort—nothing a few years of braces wouldn't fix.

"Loser," Rachel she said by way of greeting.

"Airhead," I answered back. Another Morgan smiled at Rachel as she passed us on her way to class.

"Good to see you girls are cooperating," Marsden said as he walked by. His eyes reflected the vivid orchid purple of his tie; I nearly swooned.

I watched his back disappear around the bend at the end of the hall.

"My brother's a Michael, you know. So's my dad. Same cohort as Mr. Marsden," she bragged.

"Do you ever get them confused? You know, like, want to call Marsden 'Dad'?"

She turned to face me. "Let's get one thing straight, space waste." She wagged a finger at me. "Marsden said we had to hang. He never said we had to talk." She spun on her heels and walked away. Fine auburn threads whipped my cheek.

I followed her to her locker and waited while she rummaged for her books. When she was done, she handed me an envelope. "Here," she said.

"What's this?" I asked.

"The bill. Replacement extensions. For the ones you ripped out yesterday."

"Oh," I said. I suppose I had it coming. I looked up and she was gone again. "Wait," I said, following her down the busy hall. "Where should we meet for lunch?"

Rachel paused outside the girls' room. "You wanna follow me in here, too? Hold my hand while I go?"

"Marsden said—"

"Right. Lunch. Look: I'll find you, okay?"

"Promise?"

"Do I have to?" she looked at her feet, embarrassed to be seen by the Carols and the Heathers and the Bridgets that passed us on their way in and out of the bathroom. "Look, I have no desire to get suspended or worse, so, yeah, I guess I promise."

I nodded as if to seal the deal.

"Why do you hate us so much?" I asked Rachel at lunch. She'd found me in line in the servery and used our predicament to bud.

"And by 'us' you mean..."

"Us. You know, Natural Borns."

"I don't *hate* you," she said. "I just don't like you."

"Same difference."

Rachel shrugged.

"So why?"

"I don't know."

A gaggle of Morgans and Meagans danced by, giggling.

"Look: it's no picnic belonging to a cohort. Everyone knows your year of conception and everyone knows your problems. With Naturals it's different, you know? No one knows your problems until they show."

"I'd rather know," I said, almost a whisper.

"Know when you're six that by the time you're twelve you'll lose all your hair? What about the Dereks? They need to have their gallbladders removed before their fifteenth birthdays or suffer the pain of gallstones."

"But you're all designed to be great-looking, smart, popular—"

"Like you're not any of those things?"

Had I heard her correctly? Was she jealous of me? Was Rachel—a Morgan—actually jealous of *me*? Lina, a Natural Born? Me: plain, mousy, struggles with Math Lina? "I'm not—"

"You know what? Just forget it. I'm done with this. Let Marsden do whatever he wants with me." She gathered the remnants of her lunch. "I should've known better than to think I could talk to a Natural."

I tried calling Rachel that night, but she wouldn't come to the phone. I racked my brain wondering what I'd done to peeve Rachel at lunch but could think of nothing. Imagine: a Clone jealous of a Natural. Clones ruled the world. They lived longer, looked better, and were generally more successful than Naturals. So what if some models turned out to have minor genetic errors—hair loss, diabetes, sensitivity to sunlight, lactose intolerance, severe acne—it was nothing that wasn't considered normal in the Natural population. Maybe that was the problem—when you spent that much for a genetically enhanced child, maybe you wanted something a little better than 'normal'.

I waited for Rachel in the front foyer the following day, as well. When she saw me, she rolled her eyes again. "What do you want?" she said and continued walking. I got up and followed her.

"I was thinking. About yesterday?"

Rachel turned quickly. Before I knew it, she had me pinned against the lockers. "If you say anything— anything!—about what I told you yesterday to anyone, you'll be sorry."

It took a moment for me to rise above the shock of being slammed against the wall. The lock jammed into the crook of my back. "Who would I tell?"

"I have a reputation," she whispered angrily. "I'm a Morgan. My parents designed me to be this way. I have no desire to be one of you."

"Okay," I said, trying to push her away. She flinched, then brushed her hair behind her neck with a flip. I watched people pass behind Rachel in the newly crowded hallway. A few stopped to glare, but most just kept on walking.

"We," she said, pointing a finger between us, "are not friends. We never were."

"Okay, okay," I said again.

The warning bell rang.

"I gotta go. I can't be late for class."

She left me standing against the locker, the combination lock still pressing into my back.

"Hey," a Derek said. His smile was perfect, his teeth evenly spaced and bright white. The Dereks had been bred for sports. I think this one was the lead quarterback of the school's football team. "My locker?"

It took me a moment to understand. "Sorry," I said, and went to class.

"Why did you decide to have me naturally?" I asked my parents at the dinner table that night.

"We wanted a child," my mom said.

"And we couldn't afford in vitro," Dad continued.

I thought for a moment. Mom spooned a ladle of peas onto my plate. The dreaded peas. Mushy. Soupy. Gross. Mom believed eating green vegetables would make my bones strong. I wondered if Rachel had to eat her peas or if her bone health came naturally. "Why not just wait?" I asked. "You know, till you could afford it."

"I suppose we could have done," Mom said, "but then you wouldn't be you, now would you? You'd be a Meagan or a Brittany or an Ashley. Lina would be more of a cover, a pseudonym. Deep down, you might still be my Lina, but people would never see it. To the world, you'd always be Meagan or Brittany or Ashley, never Lina."

Mom had a point. She'd almost made a believer out of me, but then I thought about my academics. "Aren't you concerned for my future? I mean, how will I ever get a job? If it's a choice between me and a Clone—"

"People were successful before cloning took hold," my dad said, "and they're still successful today. For every cloned engineer there are two Natural Born engineers."

"And all three are in competition for the same job. Cloning raised the bar. I'm just saying I don't think I'm tall enough to step over it."

Mom kissed the top of my head and sat in the seat beside mine. "So buy shoes with higher heels."

I was in bed studying when Rachel knocked on my door. "Can I come in?" she asked timidly. I hadn't heard the doorbell ring. One of my parents must've let her in.

I nodded. She closed the door behind her and sat at the foot of my bed.

"This is a surprise," I told her.

"Tell me about it." She stood and wandered around my room, checking out the things I'd saved and kept on display over the years.

She took her time spitting out whatever it was she wanted to say. "Well?" I said. "I haven't got all day." That was mean. I couldn't help it: Rachel seemed to bring out the worst in me.

"I need your help," she said. She looked at me in the mirror over my vanity, sat on the bench, and fingered the nail polish bottles and makeup compacts. "I'm tired of being a Morgan. I want to be Rachel. I want to be myself."

"So what do you want from me?"

"I figure who else knows about being themselves but you? You're the only Lina I know. You're one of a kind." She looked at herself in the mirror. "Maybe I could get contact lenses." And cover up the golden flecks in those beautiful doe-brown eyes? "Or dye my hair to be more like yours." And be mousy rather than the perfect auburn I always sworn I'd eventually change my own colour to? "What do you think?"

"What will your friends say?"

"Who cares what the other Morgans'll say? I won't be one of them anymore, remember?"

"You're sure about this?"

She looked at me through the mirror once more and nodded tentatively.

"Fine," I said. "Okay. We can start tomorrow."

I walked her down the stairs and out onto the front porch where she thanked me. "Scared?" I asked her.

"A little," she said.

We waved goodbye. I watched her walk down the front path and disappear into the darkness.

"Who was that?" Mom asked from inside the front doorway.

"Rachel."

"She's...I mean...isn't she—"

"A Morgan?"

"Uh-huh."

I shook my head. "No. She's just Rachel."

GHOST STORIES

BUBBY'S GARDEN

There's a visitor waiting for me in my garden, a slender woman with long, chestnut hair. It takes me a moment to realize this is my grand-daughter. It seems like I saw her last only yesterday, pubescent and chubby; my how fast they grow. She kneels by my garden, weeding between the flowers and pruning back the rose bush my son planted last spring. She has a heart of gold, this one, *mein sheine meidel*, my beautiful girl.

I lean against the marble ornament, a remembrance from my family a few years ago (they know how much time I spend admiring my garden), watching her. She continues to weed as if she hasn't seen me. When she's done, she wipes a bead of sweat that's trickled down her rosy cheek from her forehead, smoothes her blouse, and clears her throat. "Hi, Bubby," she says quietly. "It's me, Rachel." As if she has to tell me who she is. I'm not senile, not yet. That round face—such a *sheine punim*—those pale blue eyes, those rosy cheeks, those full lips that belonged to my husband Solly, may he rest in peace. She can't deny it, this one, she's *mien kinder*, my child, through and through.

"I just wanted to say hi, Bubby, catch up with our lives. It's been so long; I miss you." A tear forms in her eye. She blinks it away and sniffles. "I'm graduating university next week. A B.A. from the University of Toronto. Psychology. I'm thinking of becoming a therapist. Or a teacher.

"I met someone. He's really nice. His parents say they remember you from your store in Kensington Market. His grandfather used to send his father for cheese in your store every Friday before *Shabbos*, so they'd have it the next morning for breakfast. Funny what a small world this is, huh?

"His name's Brian. I think he may be the one, Bubby, my *besheret*, my soul mate. He's hinted at marriage quite a bit lately. When I was twelve and Mom took me to visit you in that hospital just after your fall? I remember that you told me you'd be okay, that you had plans to dance at my wedding. If it happens, if Brian proposes and we get married, I know you'll still be there.

"Mom says, 'Hi'. She wanted to come with me, but I told her I'd rather spend some time with you alone. She'll probably come by sometime this week."

I smile at her and open my mouth as if to speak, but she cuts me off.

"I'm pregnant, Bubby," she says with some effort. "I wanted to tell you. I wanted you to be the first to know." More tears. I reach for her hand, and she looks up, looks more *through* me than at me, as if I weren't there at all. "I know what you must be thinking—it's a *shande*, a shame, how could this happen to my grand-daughter, my *mumela*, as you used to call me.

"I don't think I can get rid of it. It's not the Jewish way." She lowers her voice until it's barely a whisper. "It's not *my* way.

"Brian'll probably want to get married."

Do you love him? I ask.

"I do love him, Bubby. And I know he loves me. I know he'll make a wonderful father."

But what about your plans? For your career? For your future?

"There's always day care, or I could wait, do my post-graduate work once the baby's old enough to go to school." She takes a tissue from her purse, dabs at her cheeks, and blows her nose.

We'll work it out, Mumela. *You'll work it out.*

"It'll be okay, Bubby. I know it will." She blows her nose once more and repositions a few flowers in my garden. "It'll be okay," she repeats.

From her pocket, Rachel takes a small stone on which she's painted a large heart overlapped by a smaller one. This is a tradition she started when she was a youngster. Every time she visits my garden she leaves me another painted stone on my marble ornament. Over time, weather has displaced some which she picks up and puts back on the slab. Others have faded or washed away with winter's run-off, lost forever. This is the true *shande*.

"I have to go now, Bubby."

I love you, my Rachel, mein *grand*-tochter.

"I love you, Bubby. And I miss you." Another tear forms at the corner of her eye which she whisks away with a finger.

I miss you, too, Mumela. Come back soon.

She turns to leave and takes a few steps toward the laneway.

Bring your Brian next time, I call after her, loathe to see her leave. Gardens can only nurture you so far before you start to get lonely for human companionship.

She turns back toward me. "Maybe I'll bring Brian next time," she says. "You'll love him, Bubby, I just know it."

I walk over to where she's standing. She's grown to be a beautiful woman, this child, *mein einekle.* She'll be a wonderful mother.

I reach out to her and brush her cheek. *I will dance at your wedding yet,* I tell her, and she smiles.

I watch as she walks to her car and climbs in. She takes a moment to compose herself before she drives off and I'm once more left alone in my garden.

THE EARL OF OSWALD'S REVENGE

On the occasion of my twenty-first birthday, I planned to recapture my birthright. It had been long-rumoured my family was descended from royalty. My great-grandfather, exiled from his homeland in his youth, arrived in Canada with a trunkful of trinkets they'd stolen, and a dream they'd realized, having bartered away most of the trinkets for materials and workers to build a palatial home in the centre of the city. History has it, my great-grandfather lost everything in the depression, and with Shakespearean flair, hanged himself from the turret, dressed in full armour, sign reading, "I shall return," strung to his neck. The bank, in time, foreclosed on the castle, rendering his family homeless paupers.

It took several generations for our family to get back on its feet. My father was the first since then to own his own home. As for my great-grandfather, he had been buried without a marker somewhere in the city, his dream home purchased for peanuts by some Gatsby recluse who, distrusting of banks, had socked his earnings away in his mattress. When he'd died intestate, the property defaulted to the Crown who sold it to someone, who had sold it to someone else, and so on. At one point, it had been rented out to frat boys for a decade who'd helped put the house on its path to demolition. To say it needed quite a bit of work after they'd vacated, was an understatement.

When I was a child, my grandfather used to drive me down to that part of the city and we'd stop in front of the house, admiring the facade which, in my mind's eye, returned to the grandeur of his youth. Grandfather had rambled for what seemed like forever about the twisting corridors and hidden passageways, about the feasts the wait-staff had served on gold-ringed plates, multi-course meals, often graced by the presence of the Rockefellers of their day. He made me promise that when I'd grown I'd purchase the carcass and return it to its former glory.

That never happened. A party planner had bought it for a song before I was even legal. But when I'd reached the age of majority, I was going to party. And I was going to do it in that house and pretend like it was mine.

The owner had restored the building, blowing out some walls (or so the web page had said) to make the smaller rooms party-sized. She made a good business hosting christenings (the web page had boasted), bar and bat mitzvahs, sweet sixteens, graduations, engagements, weddings, anniversaries, and assorted landmark birthdays, but never a coming of age party (this she told me on the phone), and never the whole house for the whole night. I told her there was a first for everything and she agreed. I agreed to pay in advance and in full and to cover any damage my guests might cause. I gave her my mother's credit card (with her knowledge—I had to sell her my first born if I defaulted even a cent on the payback), invited my friends, and arrived on the eve of my twenty-first birthday, ready to party.

Joe brought a keg, Sally the chips and dip. Koby picked up pizza and another keg. Alia made this fantastic punch that someone spiked way before the clock had struck midnight. Food and drink magically seemed to appear as the night wore on. The number of guests multiplied until the original dozen or so for which I'd planned had easily doubled, if not tripled. And, as they say, the band—or in this case, the DJ—played on.

The main room was one long room, separated into two with an arch. Granddad had said there was a walk out to the back from this room, which had been (I assumed) removed in the restoration. I looked out the back window and saw a man in a dark suit on the grass, walk out from a hidden doorway, and peer up at me. He was old, his eyes hollow. A trick of the light, I assumed, given the darkness and incessant downfall of rain. There was enough time to think, fool old man, he'll catch his death, and then lightening lit the sky. When it subsided, he was gone. I wrote him off as being the groundskeeper (surely the owner wouldn't leave a party of barely legal kids unattended for an entire night in a house that wasn't their own) and began to explore.

Cordelia tugged my arm as I passed her, pleading with me to dance. Her breath stank of vodka, her eyelids hung at half-mast, and barely, at that. I liked Cordie, and I suspected she liked me. We hadn't done much yet but awkwardly stare into each other's google-eyes until the discomfort grew too much to bear and one of us had looked away. I had planned to make that night The Night for us, let Cordie give me the birthday gift I'd remember for a lifetime, but she was drunk, and I was curious about the groundskeeper. I begged Cordie off, vowing to hook up later, and ventured down one of those winding hallways about which my grandfather had told me.

It terminated in a dead end, which was odd, so I began to press random bricks in the walls, hoping one of those secret passages would reveal itself. When it didn't, I doubled back and took another corridor, where I found a narrow stairway, leading to the basement.

Though drywalled, the narrow hallway leading off of the narrow stairway seemed gothic. It soon veered to the right to reveal a dim light ahead. I walked toward the light, past a corridor to my right, ignoring what appeared to be three figures, trying to navigate the halls. Guests of mine, perhaps, in search of a restroom. I ignored the fact each of the figures seemed have been glowing as if lit by an internal light in the darkened hall because I wanted to see where the corridor led.

It opened onto a larger, linoleum-tiled room, partially used for storage. Boxes and unused furniture had been piled against the walls in the shadows. I was drawn to the centre of the room, felt compelled to sit, and then my eyes clouded with darkness. My first impulse was to scream, but then the movie began. It was odd, like I was dreaming, yet I assure you I was fully awake. In my dream-like state, I witnessed the death of the Earl of Oswald, my great-grandfather, who, for some unknown reason had been forced to leave his homeland, only to relive his fall from grace a second time in the New World. I watched as, despondent, he sat in this very room, cinderblock walls, cement floor, and painted his last message.

He used a rather thick brush, which he swirled in a bottle of ink, then twisted against the edge of the bottle, turning and turning until the tip came to a point. His suicide letter was a work of art, and he wanted it to be remembered as such, writing in exquisite calligraphy the reason for his demise. I heard him recite it as he wrote, and felt each brush stroke as if it were the stroke of my own pen:

> My life and all I have achieved in it
> has been for naught, and by that thought I am
> sickened...

The words appeared before my veiled eyes, some letters barely sketched, some fully coloured-in. I struggled to read what else was on the paper, but the more I tried, the more the figures faded.

"Dude!" Ollie's voice broke my trance, or maybe it was the slap on my shoulder, ten times harder than it needed to be. Ollie had brought about six others with him, a mix of guys and girls, in awe of what they'd seen. "Should've told us you hired a play, man," Ollie said, baked. Hell, Ollie was *over*baked. I look up and saw the image in my dream—so did everyone else in the room, it seemed.

It was like the far side of the room had travelled back in time. A man lay on the couch, lit only by a fire in the grand fireplace. There was an oil painting of a man I recognized from my granddad's pictures as his father, the Earl of Oswald. He played with a rope he held up and in his line of sight. Strings of red and gold twisted together between his fingers to form the rope. One of the brocade drapes to the side of the mantle was drooping and I realized the rope he was holding was the drape pull, golden tassel abandoned on the area rug beside the couch.

I looked down and the inkwell had returned, so I picked up the brush and dipped it in the dark black paint, twisting it against the side of the bottle to make it thin enough for the fine brush stroke I needed, but the hairs refused to stick, so I took the brush tip between my fingers and rolled it. Slowly they began to mesh. As they entwined, so did the ends of Oswald's rope. I looked down at the painting and tried to copy the calligraphy I saw on it, but my brush began to unravel and I made a mess of the word "life".

My friends gasped and I looked up to see Oswald going out the window. The rope—which he'd tied around his neck—played quickly out and over the edge, snapping taught when it reached the end, and then again and again as Oswald presumably kicked to tighten the noose, and then it was still.

My friends, half of them stoned, the other half drunk, clapped as if they'd just seen the final act in a play. They stopped and the house grew silent, and then we heard the screams.

Frozen, at first, we passed our stares around the circle as if playing a game of hot potato with our eyes. Ollie was the first to break the circle, then Lena, then one by one the others, save me. Somehow, I don't know how, I knew what was going on. I knew it was the end, the reason why the party planner had never rented the house out overnight, why she'd left us, little more than kids, alone at night—it was because the rumours were true.

A curse had been put on the house by my great-grandfather. When he'd killed himself, it had been raining, that cliché dark and stormy night, and great-granddaddy, none other than the Earl of Oswald, had only time to pen half of his suicide note. It had been the groundskeeper that had found him and alerted the rest of the house. By the time they'd cut him down, the paint had run and most of his message had been lost, but I'd seen it. I'd seen it in my vision, clear as day:

Heed my call those with part in it.
Cursed be those whom my estate and land
have stolen. These halls I shall never leave
'til cursed revenge hath seen them bleed.

The screaming ceased.

I managed to overcome my paralysis with great effort and venture upstairs to lay eyes on the Earl of Oswald's revenge.

THE SUPERNATURAL

THE CIRCLE OF LIFE

ob clawed through the dirt covering him. When at last his hand broke through and sunlight warmed his cold flesh, he flexed his muscles, relishing the moment. Not enough time had passed for him to forget what it was like to have felt a prisoner in your own body, unable to move, mind calling out to someone, anyone, to acknowledge your presence, that you were still there, still alive somewhere inside all that flesh and bone.

He lifted his body from the cavern into which it had been buried. More memories came flooding back to his rusty brain. The rave. The dance. The lights. The sound. Ecstasy may have been involved. The music, drumbeat melting, chords congealing, synths spitting—the Man in Black had come from nowhere. His lips, painted blood red, had unfurled to form a huge grin, revealing a series of teeth tapered to points. His bifurcated tongue had slithered out to moisten his lower lip. Bob had been paralysed at the sight, able to muster no more than the occasional blink as the man had raised an open palm to his mouth and blown a fine mist of powder at him. Bob was wracked with coughs, his body doubled over. When the hacking had subsided, the Man in Black was gone. What had happened between then and the moment of his awakening had all but faded from memory.

A car whizzed past on the paved highway behind him and Bob spun a half-pirouette. His rubber legs tangled beneath him, and his head hit the ground with a hollow thump. An old pickup backfired as it passed. Bob propped his upper body on his arms and raised his head above the tall grass enough to watch the truck recede into the distance.

He worked his way to his feet and took a step toward the sound of tires on blacktop, trying to set one foot in front of the other, barely able to lift his right above the tall grass before his left threatened to buckle. No sooner had his right foot found purchase on loamy soil than his left took flight, propelled by momentum alone.

Midway to the road, his stomach rumbled. A bird chirped behind him and the churning in his belly intensified. Bob did another about face and headed back toward the tree in search of the only thing that mattered: food. He had taken a few shambling steps back along his original path when a truck jumped the shoulder at the side of the highway and cut a swath through the grass as it charged toward him.

Bob felt drawn to the noise, further attracted to the flock of gulls it had sent to flight, and resumed his shuffling gait toward it. By the time he had met the truck, his hunger had grown ravenous. He looked into the cab of the truck to stare into the gaze of the Man in Black from the rave. Before his rotting brain could make this connection, the man forced the door open, batting Bob out of the way. He climbed out of the truck, faded lips pressed into a semblance of a grin.

Food! Bob's stomach and mind shouted in choral refrain. *Must eat,* they cried in broken harmony.

The man stepped from behind the truck door. Bob pounced, arms outstretched, hoping to use the weight of his body to pin the man between himself and the truck, crack his skull, and feast, but the man caught Bob's wrists with his hands and held him at bay.

Bob felt blazing hunger in his belly and set his sights on the man's jugular. He got near enough to smell coffee on his breath before the man's brick made contact with the side of Bob's head and Bob went down. He blinked, eyes focussing on the grass in front of him and the loamy soil beneath, then he felt himself being lifted as if weightless, carried as if flying, and tossed as if rotting garbage into the bed of the truck.

The man looped a chain, first around Bob's left foot and then around his right, and secured both to the bed of the truck.

Bob 's stomach roared. *Feed me!* his fetid soul cried.

He could smell the man, acrid and spicy on the surface, sinew and salty on the inside.

Meat! his appetite yearned.

The man swung the chain around Bob's right wrist and Bob pounced, teeth sinking into the flesh of the man's neck. Bob tasted blood. He pulled away and bit once more. Tearing at the skin beneath the man's ear, he pulled a piece free from the bone and chewed.

The man screamed. He tried to hold Bob off, to keep his teeth at bay by planting a palm on Bob's forehead. Bob grabbed at the man's midsection, pulled him as close as he could, and gorged on the meat of his stomach.

The man beat against Bob's back for a moment or two before his life slipped from him.

Bob's teeth jerked toward the man again, missed their target, and jerked again. The action set the man's body to motion and it rolled from the bed of the truck and onto the grass below.

Freshly ignited, Bob's bloodlust demanded more. His belly complained. Bob roared. He struggled against his chains but they held fast. He lay back against the metal of the truck bed, feeling his hunger grow.

The first carrion landed less than an hour later. It perched on Bob's chest and pecked at his hand. Famished beyond starvation, Bob lunged for it. The bird fluttered its wings and re-lit on Bob's chest. Its beak picked off one of Bob's shirt buttons and then pecked at the fetid flesh beneath the gaping cloth. It stopped once, briefly, to caw and then continued ravaging Bob's remains.

ΛT THE MERE THOUGHT OF

Crane stepped into the hotel's glass-enclosed elevator, pressed "L" for lobby, and looked out at the view. By the time he realized he was on his way up instead of down, it was too late. The curse he'd meant to utter fell short on his tongue and he was drawn back to the view. The sun shone bright yellow in the midst of an azure sky, the expanse broken only by random coral reminders of daybreak; it was going to be a beautiful day.

When at last the elevator stopped and the doors parted it was to a flurry of activity. A pair of paramedics, one male, one female, thrust a teenager on a stretcher past him. Crane gave them wide berth, wedging himself into the far corner.

The girl wore an oxygen mask and an IV in her arm. She grabbed the paramedic's shirt sleeve and mumbled incoherently. Gently, the male EMT removed her hand from his elbow, tucked it under the orange blanket draped over the stretcher, and tightened the girl's restraints. The woman cooed in an effort to calm the girl.

A wasp buzzed against the glass and then came to rest on the sill near the floor. The male EMT startled and took a step back. He smiled, surprised at his discomfort. "Wasps," he said.

The woman nodded politely.

The man chuckled and explained to Crane, "When I was young, I was stung by one, by a wasp. Hurt like there was no tomorrow. Tried to steer clear of the little bastards ever since."

The woman smiled. Crane allowed his attention to divert back to the sky. The coral had thinned until it was as wispy as the clouds.

"Silly, huh?" the EMT continued. "It's so small, so vulnerable. I could just..." he raised his foot until it hovered over the insect in contemplation of bringing his shoe down on it. "That something so small could make me break out into a cold sweat..."

Crane watched as the wasp bounded between the glass, the window sill, and the sole of the EMT's shoe, watched as it appeared to spar with its reflection, and struggled to escape through the glass. Crane listened to the incessant buzz of the beating wings, tinny, almost mechanical, stopping only momentarily as it paused to recover each time it flew head on into the glass.

Crane grew restless. He leaned toward the button panel. "Damn, these elevators are slow." He reached over the girl to press the button and she grabbed his hand.

"The toys are alive!' she said, panic in her voice.

Crane struggled to free his hand, but her grip was strong.

"They're coming! The green army men! That sound! Their helicopter! It's going to crash into the elevator!"

At last, Crane worked his hand free. It tingled as if the wasp had spent time beating its wings against the skin there. He rubbed it as he looked, embarrassed, at the EMTs.

"Babysitter," the woman explained. "Claims a rag-doll attacked her." She cast a sympathetic glare at the girl.

"On something, probably," the man added. "Shame when it happens to someone so young."

The wasp hummed as it hovered between the glass wall of the elevator and the floor.

The elevator doors opened at last. Crane ducked as the wasp flew over his shoulder, and then over the shoulders of the EMTs as they hustled the girl off the elevator.

Crane stepped out of the elevator and into the warmth of the sunlight. The wasp hovered around his head. Crane batted it away, shoved his hands into his pockets, bowed his head, and walked toward his car with purpose, worried he'd be late for his morning meeting.

"What's going on?" the girl on the stretcher demanded. "Where am I?" her voice forceful and coherent. She fought against her restraints as the EMTs attempted to calm her.

The wasp encircled his head again, this time joined by another. And then another. Crane drew the collar of his jacket closer around his neck, bowed his head further, and walked faster. The wasps followed, dark as a storm cloud. His own personal storm cloud. They hummed incessantly, buzzing louder than his morning alarm.

Crane quickened his pace. He batted the wasps out of the way as they lit on his nose, his forehead, flew underneath his glasses, and then stung.

He began to run, arms propelling him forward as they pin-wheeled the wasp-darkened sky. Though Crane had been nearly blinded by the swarm about his head, he paused for a moment to search for help. He was able to make out a man reading on a bench in a park in the distance. The man folded his paper and stood as Crane approached. "Killer wasps!" Crane managed. A wasp flew into his mouth. Its bristles prickled his tongue. He sputtered it out. "Swarm!" Crane continued. "Save yourself!"

Crane dropped to the floor and began to roll. If he couldn't outrun the little buggars, maybe he could squash a few of them before they got the better of him.

"There's nothing there, man!" the man said. He grabbed for Crane's hand and fought to help him stand.

Crane blinked; the wasps were gone.

"Do you hear that?" the man asked. He rubbed his hand as if he'd been stung himself.

The man looked to the sun, shielding his eyes with his hand. "My God," he said, "it's true!"

Crane brushed the grass from his suit. He checked the sky to make sure the wasps had gone and saw nothing but a bright, white sun, framed by a clear, peacock blue sky.

"Don't you see it?" the man asked.

Crane parroted the trajectory of the man's gaze. Outside of a few, thin clouds, he saw nothing.

"The asteroid! It's coming!" He took a few steps backward and nearly tripped over the bench. "That sound! It's deafening!" He held his hands over his ears as he stared in horror at the sky. "We have to warn people!" He took hold of Crane's jacket at the lapels, one in each hand. "We have to warn them!" Crane watched as the man darted across the park and into the distance.

At Crane's feet, on the grass, lay the man's newspaper. He picked it up, meaning to return it to the man, but he was nothing more than a speck in the distance. Crane skimmed the article the man had been reading, something about an asteroid on a crash collision with Earth.

The whine of an ambulance struck up, muted by the distance. A single wasp blew by his ear and then was gone, taken by the breeze. Crane looked to the sky and breathed deeply. It was going to be a beautiful day.

THE LAST SUPPER

"**Y**ou have to invite me in. That's the rule. I'm kinda bound by it."

"Chad?"

"Yeah, Ma, it's me. Can I come in?"

She nodded and opened the door wider.

"You have to say the words or I can't come in."

"Huh? Oh. Yes. Come in." She blinked and closed the door. Her eyes followed him as he entered the room.

"I can't stay for long, Ma, only about six more hours to sunlight."

"Of course," she nodded.

She took a breath as if to speak, but he continued instead: "Even the slightest bit of sun, they tell me, and poof! Game over."

"You look pale, so pale." She reached a tentative hand to his cheek. "And cold, so cold."

"Death kind of does that to a person, Ma." He sat down on the overstuffed easy chair.

"Death. Of course." She sat down on the ottoman in front of him. He was picking at the threads on the arms of the chair again. How like him. And yet...

And yet it couldn't possibly be him. He had died exactly one week ago to the day. She had buried him, five long days ago; the condolence food was still rotting in the fridge.

"How? How could...but you're...you're..."

"Dead? No, not dead—undead."

"Chad, I...what?"

"Undead. Like Dracula. Like the dudes Buffy slays. Like Angel, you know...a vamp."

"A what?"

"A vamp. You know, a vampire? Nosferatu?"

"Chad..." She paused, "Chad. You can't seriously expect me to believe..."

"What, Ma? What? That you buried me? That here I am again, today, on the one week anniversary of my death?"

She nodded.

"Well, here I am. Here I am in the...in the flesh."

She looked down at her hands writhing in her lap. So now what, she thought, now what? Does life just go on? Go on as normal? Like nothing ever happened? Like he'd never...left in the first place? She sighed, looked up at him, and smiled. "Your room. I kept it the same. It's as if you never left."

"God, you're so melodramatic sometimes; it's only been a week. Besides, I can't stay long. I already told you: sunlight? Poof? Remember?"

"Don't be silly, Chad. A little sun does a body good."

"Not this body, Ma. I told ya: sizzle and poof."

"Where will you go? Who will take care of you? How will I know you're okay?"

"I'm not okay, Ma. I told ya. I'm a vampire; I'll never be okay again.

"Besides, I'm a part of a pack now. We hang in the subway. Have to avoid the grates, though."

"Poof, right?"

"You got it."

"So, are they nice? These people you hang out with? Your...your pack."

"Nice enough, I guess. For people who kill people."

"Kill?"

"Well, not always. But most of the time, yeah."

"Chad, you've always been such a nice boy. These people...your pack...can't you find someone else to hang out with? Tommy, for instance. He's missed you so much since you've gone."

Chad laughed. "Tommy's still alive; I'm dead, remember?"

"Undead."

"Whatever! Look, Tommy's a nice guy and all, but he's got that whole human thing going for him, that...warm-blooded thing. I'd literally be all over him in no time."

"But Chad, killing? You couldn't harm a fly."

"Oh, Ma, it's different now. Way different.

"Besides, I really don't have to kill. There are these places a guy can go where people actually let you drink their blood...for a price."

"Prostitutes?"

"Naw, not hookers...they don't sell sex. Just blood."

"But still...And this blood, you...drink...it?"

"Of course. How else?"

"But...aren't you afraid?"

"Of what? I'm ten times stronger now. I can take care of myself. Miss the whole heart beating thing, though."

"No, I mean...aren't you afraid of AIDS...and things...disease?"

"It's not like it can kill me or anything. I'm already dead, remember?"

"Yes, of course, I remember. Please stop reminding me. I remember, okay. I remember you're dead. That's why you're sitting right there. I'm talking to a corpse."

"Always with the irony, huh, Ma? I should've known. I should've never come. Not to you." He stood up.

She grabbed his arm at the wrist. For the first time since his arrival, they made eye contact. His pupils were red. He looked just like the last photographs she'd taken of him: pale with red-eye. She never had been much of a photographer. "Please don't go."

They maintained eye contact. In his eyes, eyes that had been warm and wet and brown in life, she saw pain and torture. She refused to blink, staring into his eyes, looking for the one thing she knew would set things right, the one thing that would bring him back to her in the end. But all she saw was cold, pain, torture, and hunger. Hunger not for love, to be loved, but for blood. At that moment she knew he had been lost forever; her son was gone.

"I just came to say goodbye. I can't stay."

"Please, stay. For a little while. Sun doesn't come up these days until at least seven. It's barely one."

"I gotta go, Ma. I'm hungry."

"I've got plenty of food in the fridge. There was a funeral; people always bring food to a funeral."

"I don't eat much solid food nowadays."

"Right. The whole blood thing."

"Right." He sat down again. "Well, I guess I could stay just a little while longer."

"No, you're right. You should go. Go eat something."

"But I..."

"Unless..."

"Huh?"

"Unless you could feed off me."

"What? I...no! No way!"

"Why not? I could be like those people you talked about earlier."

"I couldn't, Ma. No way!"

"What? It's not like you've never done it before. Six long months I nursed you; you didn't seem to mind back then."

"Huh? That's gross, Ma! Gross!" He stood up and backed away.

"Think about it, Chad. Just stop a second and think: I'm your mother. I love you." She rolled up her sleeve and held her inner elbow out to him. "Here, Chad. Take it. Take my blood."

"Stop it, will ya? Just stop! I'm not drinking from you and that's final."

"But Chad..."

"No! No way." Once more, they looked into each other's eyes. He had changed, she noticed. His ears were pointier, and as he breathed his mouth opened and she noticed his incisors had grown to razor sharpness, twice their original length. She shuddered at the thought of those teeth burying themselves in the delicate flesh of her inner arm and rolled down her sleeve.

"Well," she muttered.

"Well."

"Well, well, well." She laughed a nervous titter.

"Well, I guess I really should be going now."

"Can I at least give you some money?"

"I don't need any, Ma." He smiled. "I'll be fine."

"It's just that...well..." She retreated to the front door to get her purse. "You said there are people who sell their blood," she fumbled for her wallet, "and I just thought..."

He reached out to stay her hand. She started at his clammy touch. "I'll be fine." He smiled again. "Really, I promise."

"Chad, I just don't know, I..."

"Really, I promise. I'll be fine.

"Goodbye, Ma," he said as his teeth found her jugular. "Thanks for dinner."

LEATHER BAT

The yard or so of black leather rose into the air, gliding on the wind. It swooped and swayed over the cars, giant bat with an impossible wingspan, threatening to dive at any moment. It floated briefly in front of her vehicle, as if deciding to attack the windshield or fly away. Her foot hovered over the brake. She checked the rear-view mirror— she was free of tailgaters. Still, it remained airborne as it drifted to the right, able to negotiate the breeze as it came to land between the lanes on the blacktop.

Mystified by its ability to mimic life, she drove on.

THE NEXUS

The flyers for The Gateway Fellowship had the knack of popping up around campus in the least likely of places. Printed on bright, neon-colored paper and depicting their logo—three heavy, dark, interconnected circles, like a truncated Olympics symbol—underlined with Gateway's slogan: "Things will never be the same". At first, they were hung on utility posts and stapled to bulletin boards, but eventually, as whatever it was caught on, it graduated to binders and even t-shirts. Trouble was, no one really knew what the symbol represented, nor what The Gateway Fellowship was, at least, if they did, they weren't talking. It was weird, ominous—like the copy for some B horror flick. But to a generation that had been weaned on the media, cut their teeth on conspiracy theories, and lived in the shadow of Armageddon, ominous was cool and Gateway caught on and stuck.

It was almost a full month after I saw my first poster that I discovered the agenda Gateway had to offer.

My name is Molly McBride. I'm a professor of Archaeology at the University of Toronto. My specialty is Historic Archaeology, studying the remains of the last two hundred years or so; my *passion* is Pseudo-Archaeology, extrapolating explanations for seemingly inexplicable finds, such as the final resting place of Noah's Ark, or the current resting place of the Holy Grail. When I first received Josef Schliemann's invitation to visit the site of the old Jesuit Mission—reputed to have been a source of great power for Iroquois living in the area more than five centuries ago, which also happened to be the new headquarters for the Gateway Fellowship—I was psyched, though wary. Josef Schliemann was a less than savory character who made his living sensationalizing archaeology. Schliemann's the guy that's quoted in all the tabloids as "expert", first on the lists of willing "scientists", for producers of shows documenting the paranormal and the unexplained. He'd sign his name to any assertion so long as it got his name in print. Especially if there were a cheque to go with it.

The mere thought of taking a meeting alone with Schliemann, angered my husband, Palmer Richardson. He knows all about Schliemann; they have a history. He'd always suspected more was going on at Gateway than an alternative to dorm life, though this was the first time he'd ever put Gateway and Schliemann together. Palmer insisted I forget I ever saw the note, but curiosity eventually won over and I was determined to check it out.

Gateway was a majestic stone structure, framed by a grassy field known as Gateway Park. Hailed as the oldest building in the city, the church was built by the Jesuits themselves. The Mission is testament to the life of one man: Henri Archambault, a Jesuit priest sent to Upper Canada to "civilize" the natives. Archambault was said to have organized and oversaw the building of the structure, single-handedly. It saw services under its roof until the structure was damaged in a storm in the late nineteen-eighties. The walls were fortified and the property fenced-in until it was sold last year. After a hasty renovation, the old Jesuit Mission became the home of the new Gateway Fellowship.

A young man wearing a powder-blue, Roots hoodie and blue jeans met me at the oversized, gothic-style door and gave me the grand tour—great hall; meeting room; commissary; dormitory. Students, some of which I recognized from campus, milled about in the poorly ventilated, barely lit corridors. Others socialized in the great hall, studied in the commissary, or were in the process of moving personal possessions into the dorms. The tour ended in front of the rector's office. Powder-blue Hoodie knocked once on the heavy, wooden door and pushed it open to reveal Josef Schliemann, beaming at me from behind a large wooden table. He looked just as I'd remembered, except a bit gaunter, as though he had lost too much weight. He wore a long-sleeved, black t-shirt which hung on his broad frame. His hair was cut so short it was more like stubble, which did nothing to hide the fact that his hairline had receded considerably since we'd last met. Around his neck, hanging from a diamond-cut gold chain, was a charm in the shape of the symbol that had come to symbolize his organization: three interlocked rings.

"Molly," he shouted, as if we were long lost friends, "good to see you." We shook hands, he grabbing my hand in both of his. "Please. Sit," he said. His outstretched hand indicated what looked like an over-stuffed, Edwardian wing-tip opposite him. "It's been a while, hasn't it, Moll?" he said.

I tried to get comfortable on the rock-hard seat cushion. "Quite the set-up you have here, Josef."

"Do you like it?"

"That all depends on what 'it' is."

85

"My own personal empire."

I looked at him, then, trying to gauge his sincerity. "You're serious, aren't you?"

"The Fellowship is my baby. I created it."

"How nice for you."

He smiled a self-satisfying grin.

The silence that followed was uncomfortably thick. "So really: what is this place?" I asked.

"Think of us as an alternative campus life concentrated in one building rather than spread out over the downtown core. A home away from home."

"For a price."

He closed his eyes and bowed his head, allowing me the concession. "Do you not also pay to live where you live?"

I had no answer for him. Rumors surrounding Gateway and its doctrine were as conflicting as they were abundant. Most accounts agreed it was either a cult of the ancients or a cult of personality. Knowing what I knew about Schliemann, I was betting on the latter. Students paid exorbitant fees to bask in the presence that was Josef Schliemann; it was almost obscene.

"So what," I said, finally thinking of something to say, "students can stay here as long as they check their worldly possessions at the door? Fork over their allowance and tuck money and anything else Mom and Dad are willing to send by way of Western Union?" I was baiting him, I know I was, but I was hoping that if I could put him on edge, he might give up a little more information than he'd planned.

"Come on, Molly. You of all people should know better than to reduce what I've built here to a cliché."

"Okay. So...enlighten me."

He shook a single finger at me. "Interesting you use that word: enlighten, for this is what we hope to do at Gateway: enlighten people to the fact there is a higher spirit in the world. That all things in Nature are sacred. That all people, being of Nature, should be revered as sacred."

The longer I sat there staring into his smarmy face, feeling his smugness wash over me in waves, the more my skin crawled. "Cut to the chase, Josef," I told him. "I haven't got all day. What do you want, for me to join your cult?"

He smirked and tilted his head, a nonchalant gesture that said, "Why not."

"Goodbye, Josef," I said, standing. I turned and walked toward the door. Powder-blue Hoodie blocked my egress. If there was one thing that could be said about Josef Schliemann, it was that he had his monkeys well-trained. "Excuse me," I said over the sound of Schliemann's chair scraping on the hardwood floor as he raced to get out from behind his desk.

"Molly, please," Schliemann said as he touched my elbow and tugged gently. "I have some real business to discuss."

I turned to look at him.

"Please?" he asked. Something in the way he'd said it sounded genuine. Reluctantly, I allowed myself to be led back to the wingtip chair.

"You are familiar with the history of this building, I suppose?"

I nodded. "Vaguely."

"Legend has it that when the missionaries came to this place, they discovered a stone altar, close to this very spot. The natives they found insisted it was a spiritual place. Their word for the altar roughly translated to 'gateway', hence the name of Gateway Park. In Latin, the missionaries translated it as 'nexus'.

"Henri Archambault, one of the missionaries, kept detailed logs of his attempts to 'civilize' the natives." He used his index and middle fingers to punctuate his head as he said the word 'civilize'. "It was he behind the push to build the original church on this location, to show them another flavor of spirituality.

"Archambault was a bit of a radical, branded as a heretic by the Church. Had he stayed in his native France, he would have been excommunicated within a month. When he volunteered to join the expedition to the Canadas, his superiors endorsed the decision—probably figured good riddance to bad rubbish, no?"

Schliemann sat on his desk at an angle. One foot dangled shorter than the other.

"Archambault was left to oversee the natives but became enchanted with their spirituality before long. Ironically, it was they who eventually 'civilized' him. He lived amongst the natives as an equal, even taking himself a wife, which as you know, is strictly *verboten* for a priest.

"After spending ten years in the Canadas, Archambault was forced by his peers to return to France, but he did so a changed man. Spouting non-sequiturs about having witnessed living, breathing gods and flying chariots, he vowed to return to the land and the people he had grown to love so dearly. Archambault was institutionalized where he spent out the remainder of his days, abandoned by his family and peers.

"Upon embarkation of the ship that would return him from his mission to enlighten the civil world regarding the ostensible savages populating the Canadas back in 1791, Archambault proclaimed, 'There are more things in heaven and earth than modern man will ever know or understand.' Pretty bold words for a man reputed to have been dragged aboard in shackles, no?

"What they failed to realize—what they *all...failed*...to realize—was that Archambault was a visionary, on par with DaVinci and Nostradamus. He had the uncanny knack for prognostication. The Church was probably more afraid of him than anything else."

He held out a pile of paper for me. "What's this?" I asked.

"Proof positive of Archambault's genius."

I took the bundle and flipped through it; I think I was frowning as I did, because Schliemann said, "Still skeptical, eh?" He rifled through more paper on his desk before handing me a second pile. "Read it for yourself." He pointed at the pile of paper in my hand. "Xeroxes of Archambault's work, in the original French.

"Archambault was quite the inventor. He has blueprints for the most mundane—and the most wondrous—of contraptions in there. Everything from an inextinguishable power source to mechanical flying devices. In case you're wondering, I've already checked the North American patent offices. Turns out, I'm the first to register the designs."

"Where did you get this?"

"I was hired by the French to catalogue a portion of their archival material. There are reams and reams of documents—valuable, historical documents—that no one but myself—and now you—knows about. No one else in the world."

"You stole it?"

"I *have* it. Let's say I'm holding it *in trust* for the French."

"You stole it."

"If they want it back, all they have to do is ask."

I could think of nothing more to say. In giving me this information, Schliemann was giving me a reason to trust him. I soothed myself with the understanding that, should Schliemann ever fall out of line, I could turn this evidence over to the police. I suppressed a smile at the idea, even as I shook my head in disbelief.

"Oh, come on now. It's not like they'll miss the journal, or even find a use for it."

That was it. I'd had my fill of Josef Schliemann for one evening. Hell, I'd had enough of him for a lifetime. Part of the doctorate of archaeology is to foster a respect for the historic record. In taking Archambault's journal, Schliemann had spit on the holiest of holy of archaeological tenets.

"Where's all this going? Why have you brought me here?" We exchanged glances. "Make it good, Josef. You have exactly five seconds and then I'm leaving."

"Archambault built catacombs under this building. Under most of the park, in fact. One of these catacombs dead ends in what he called, 'The Chamber of the Nexus', Archambault's Fortress of Solitude, if you will—"

I looked at my watch. "Four seconds."

Schliemann continued, undaunted. "It was his office and his workshop, both. Archambault chose the location because it was directly under the sacred altar—"

"Three."

"I have discovered this chamber, and I want you to mount an archaeological excavation there. I want you to find the altar and anything else you can about Archambault himself."

"Why? So I can give your new religion credence? Give it a history? Maybe make it more authentic."

"Religion," he pooh-poohed, "Molly, Molly, Molly. Please. You give me more credit than I deserve." He flashed me a wide grin, meant to ingratiate me, I suppose; it didn't work. "I want nothing more than to bring the history of this place to the public, Molly. Make a living museum of it."

"And if you make a few bucks in the process?"

He exaggerated a frown and shrugged his shoulders. "I make a few bucks, the city makes a few bucks...This is what capitalism is all about, is it not?"

At that precise moment, as if on cue, we heard, "Let me in there you son of a bitch!" I recognized the voice.

Schliemann nodded at Powder-blue Hoodie who stepped aside, and Palmer spilled in. He took a moment to regain his composure. "Joey," he said, addressing Schliemann rather coldly.

"Paulie," Schliemann returned, amused.

Like I said before, Palmer and Schliemann have a history. They were digging on sites together back when I was still in junior high. Their relationship was affable, yet adversarial, based on a shared sense of dislike and one-upmanship. The whole "Joey"/"Paulie" thing was borne out of a mutual desire to piss the other off. Unfortunately for them, the names stuck, the fad spreading until everyone on every site they'd ever worked on had called them by those names.

"Molly?" Palmer asked.

"I'm okay. I was just leaving."

"Think about it, Moll," Schliemann said; Palmer frowned.

"Goodbye, Josef," I said. Palmer rested his arm on my shoulder and I allowed myself to be led out of the room.

Outside of the building, Palmer let go of me and walked ahead until he reached the car. I followed closely, called his name a few times, trying to get his attention, but all he said was, "Not now," and, "In the car."

He opened my door with the remote, and we climbed inside. There we sat, me taking chance glances at Palmer, trying to gauge his level of ire, and he, sitting in silence, grasping the steering wheel until his knuckles had turned white. At last, he spoke. "A cult, Molly? A cult. You just walk into the headquarters of the newest and fastest growing cult in the city as though it were City Hall. What were you thinking?"

"I was just curious. That's all."

"And after I told you I wasn't happy about it."

"You said you weren't happy, not that you didn't want me to go."

"Have you forgotten what happened the last time we teamed up with him? He held you at gunpoint. He would have finished you off right then if he wasn't distracted. Good thing he pawned you off onto one of his incompetent lackeys or I'd be sitting here talking to myself."

"It's just that I get him, okay? I get him. He's out to make a fast buck at any cost and come out smelling like roses with the world kissing his feet."

"That makes him dangerous."

"It makes him *human*. He's not a criminal mastermind. He's just a man."

"What's your part supposed to be in all of this?"

"There's a site beneath the Jesuit mission. Josef thinks there's a sacred artifact buried there, one that will give credence to his doctrine."

"So he can bring more sheep into his flock? Why would you want to be part of that?"

"The mission's the oldest building in the city, Palmer. The only thing we know about it is what the missionaries wrote in their journals. This is a chance to prove or disprove history, maybe make some history of our own. I want you to be a part of that with me."

Palmer thought about it for a moment. He smiled. "All right. Someone's got to be there to protect you when Joey's ego gets the better of him."

"And they say chivalry is dead."

He smiled at me, and cupped my cheek in his hand, leaned forward, and kissed me gently. "There *is* one condition, though: promise me you'll be careful."

I nodded and kissed him again.

"I mean it, Moll. Promise."

"Okay. I promise."

Six weeks later, I'd assembled my crew and held the permit for excavation of the Gateway site, in spite of Palmer's misgivings about the project. I spent those six weeks mired in Archambault's journals, struggling through the original French at first, comparing snippets of fragmented English from translation web sites to Schliemann's. When I was finally convinced his translations were accurate, I switched to Schliemann's version exclusively.

Archambault's journals were composed of disjointed vignettes that coloured a collage of experience. After the first year of strong-arming the natives' indoctrination into Christianity, Archambault was left behind to minister his congregation until the missionaries' return, a decade hence. Archambault was more humanitarian than dictator, allowing the natives to gradually reclaim their original way of life under his leadership.

Plagued by strange dreams, Archambault eventually sought out the guidance of the band's spiritual leader. In his journals, Archambault documented his dreams. He told of horseless carriages that belched thick, black smoke into the air; elongated, silver bullets full of people that travelled underground; and mammoth birds that expelled parallel streamers of steam in their wake, growling as they flew overhead. In his dreams, the landscape was marred by mountainous structures that gleamed in the sunlight; bright spots of yellow fire that glowed without flame; and books with lighted pages and fluid type. Cars, subways, and airplanes; skyscrapers, city lights and tablets—if I hadn't known better, I'd have sworn he'd nailed a pretty accurate description of modern-day Toronto.

And it didn't end there—page upon page of blueprints for amazing, mechanical contraptions, everything from flush toilets to electric lights, from mechanical vehicles to perpetual motion machines, and—what is perhaps even more fantastic—from teleportation devices to time machines. All close to more than five hundred years ago! Though it could have been written off as science fiction—no more than what Huxley or Wells had done a couple of hundred or so years later—Archambault's accounts were authentic enough to worry the Jesuits and make a believer of Schliemann and his growing band of followers.

Archambault lived amongst the natives for the better part of a decade. As the time for his return grew near, he orchestrated the construction of more subterranean ceremonial chambers, what Schliemann had referred to as "catacombs". The plan was to move the entire village—including the nexus—temporarily underground, so that, upon the missionaries' return, they would find nothing more than the abandoned shell of the church and the wooden longhouse structures and leave, allowing Archambault to live out the remainder of his days, unfettered by the constraints of the Church.

During the excavation, Archambault was once again afflicted with dreams, horrible dreams, in which he saw himself bound and tortured, starved and beaten, and left in a darkened room to live out the remainder of his days.

The Jesuits arrived earlier than expected and strong-armed a native into revealing Archambault's whereabouts. Horrified by the life Archambault had chosen to lead, they bound him in shackles and dragged him back to France where he was immediately institutionalized. The Church tried everything, including exorcism, but eventually branded him insane, excommunicated him, and left him to die while incarcerated.

On the whole, the journals were fascinating. How could I resist excavating the subterranean ceremonial chambers of the likes of Archambault? Six weeks seemed like an eternity before getting a project like that going, but the wait bought me time in which to soften Palmer to the idea. By the time we'd broken ground, I'd managed to convince him that, if our students were ever to experience archaeology hands-on that year, we had no other choice but to take Schliemann up on his offer.

The interior of the catacombs was a marvel of engineering. Though constructed almost five centuries ago, the heavy-hewn arched structures holding the ground above at bay were nothing short of miraculous. Schliemann led us directly to Archambault's Chamber of the Nexus, and left, as per the condition of strict, non-interference on his part, imposed by my husband—who also happened to be my department head— if he were to allow the dig to proceed.

The chamber itself was roughly square, with a hard packed, earthen floor and grey parget walls, covered with charcoal drawings. One graphic depicted an array of cloaked men wielding cruciforms like swords; another depicted a single, cloaked, cruciformed figure, surrounded by men in Native American garb. It was easy to track the progress of the solitary cloaked figure through the tableau as, though his dress had changed, the cruciform remained on his body. The graphics showed this figure—assumedly Archambault—as he assimilated into the group, married, and rallied the locals to excavate the caverns beneath the church. Lastly, the wall depicted the return of the cruciform-wielding cloaks as they dragged a bound Archambault to his doom. One scene, however, ordered between the former and the latter described here, offered new insight into the missionary's story, and that was one depicting Archambault, stone altar beneath his feet. The Archambault-figure's hands were raised to the ceiling as men on bended knee with bowed heads surrounded him in reverence. But among all of the drawings, the ones most prevalent within the chamber were the ones depicting three, interconnected circles—the mark of the Gateway Fellowship.

I assigned two members of my team to document the wall art, first with photographs, and then with measured drawings, while the remainder of my crew demarcated a grid over the area.

Excavation was slow-going. The air inside the chamber was humid, making breathing difficult at best. The sweat and body heat of ten souls scraping away at the soil did nothing to help our cause. Few artifacts were found. Those that were, seemed to be ceremonial in nature:

fragments of clay pipe molded in effigy to the human form; copper bowls pounded into shape with stone tools and etched either with a cruciform or the mark of The Gateway Fellowship; and a carved, wooden crucifix, still attached to a leather thong.

To say we dug for several days would be a misnomer; we sliced more than dug. The soil was compact and moist and came away from our trowels more like slivers of banana peel than loam. I retired to sleep each night the moment I closed my eyes, ice pack still bound to the wrist of my trowel hand, dirt that refused to be washed away impacted beneath my fingernails and blackening my knees as if tattooed there.

Day four. I was excavating one of twenty, evenly spaced, evenly sized, square units in the floor of Archambault's Chamber of the Nexus, almost a foot deep. At that depth, the soil was not as compact as the earth above. I was contemplating whether or not I'd found sterile soil, listening to the members of my crew converse, digging in silence, laughing at their periodic silliness, when I scraped something hard. It jarred me, sending a jolt through my already throbbing wrist, dissipating only mildly as it travelled past my elbow to my shoulder. I fumbled in my kit bag for a whisk-broom and continued to excavate, gently coaxing the artifact I'd found from its centuries old grave. Palmer joined me eventually, and the two of us managed to clear most of the large, circular stone that disappeared into the wall of my unit.

Palmer grabbed a shovel and quickly excavated the adjacent unit while I began to map the exposed portion of the feature. By the time we were done, most of the crew had gathered around us, facilitating the excavation by sifting through Palmer's discarded dirt.

We gazed at the circular monolith we'd uncovered, all of us, all ten of us, rendered speechless. The "monolith" had been carved from deep grey stone. We measured it; it was perfectly circular, three feet in diameter. A single, concentric circle had been left in the centre of the stone, giving it the profile of a double-tiered wedding cake. The surface of both the central platform and the outer ring appeared smooth, save for chisel marks left behind by the craftsman with one exception: three interconnected circles—the symbol of The Gateway Fellowship—repeated four times, evenly spaced, like the points of a compass.

We stood there gaping at each other in silence for quite some time, Palmer and I and the members of my crew, not quite knowing what to make of the find. There we were, archaeologists hired by the Grand Master of The Gateway Fellowship to excavate a hidden chamber beneath his temple upon which every nook and cranny appeared branded with his logo, a definite chicken or egg scenario. While I had no idea what to think (though I supposed Schliemann could have adopted the symbol after having seen it plastered on the walls of the chamber), Palmer was positive Schliemann had orchestrated the whole thing to garner publicity and draw more unsuspecting plebs into his ranks. In haste, he sent one of the crew to summon Schliemann into the chamber.

Schliemann arrived promptly, a gaggle of his followers in tow, smugness worn over his entire body like a cloak. His necklace, the one depicting the same symbol plastered on virtually every surface of the room, found what little light there was and cast starbursts on the walls, floor, and ceiling. "So?" He clapped his hands together and waited for me to make eye contact. "Talk to me, Moll," he said.

Palmer clicked his tongue and rolled his eyes in a gesture that said, "Oh, brother!" It was a sentiment I echoed. One-on-one, Schliemann wasn't so bad. It was his public persona and all that posturing that got to me every time I saw him, always that insipid need to feel important, to be superior. Probably why he took to pandering for the media so often. I decided to ignore the attitude. "This," I said, standing, pointing to the stone platform with a single steel-toed work boot. "I wonder, Josef," I said, leaping across the feature until I faced him, "what do you make of it?"

"Yeah, *Josef*," Palmer challenged, "what do *you* make of it?"

Schliemann side-stepped me so he could study the find. At first, he just stood there, rubbing his chin with his hand. Then he squatted beside it, tracing the glyphs on its face with his fingers, while his followers milled about, whispering to each other. When at last he spoke, it came out as a whisper. "It's the altar," he said. He cleared his throat, stood, and said it once more, "It's the altar," he bellowed, "the gateway of legend." At this point, he turned to face his flock, "Behold!" He raised his hands to the sky, then lowered them slightly, having to make a minor adjustment as his fingers scraped the ceiling of the chamber. "Behold the Nexus!"

The twenty-or-so of us crammed into the chamber stared at each other in anti-climactic silence for what seemed like a very long time until—at last—the silence was broken by the sound of a single person clapping. The claps had been muffled, sound waves absorbed by the porous walls and low-hanging roof, but they were still loud enough to get our attention. We all turned in the direction of the noise-maker; I was mortified to learn it was Palmer. "Okay, so you got our attention," he addressed Schliemann. "Now what? Spirits materializing from the sky? Archambault's return? I know: the whole building crumbles in on itself and is swallowed up by the underworld."

"He who rules the Nexus rules the world, Paulie," Schliemann said, almost too calmly.

"Is that a fact?"

"Yes, Paulie," Schliemann answered, distracted, "that's a...it's a fact."

"Well by my calculations, seeing as Molly here holds the excavation license, I'd say she's currently the one who rules the Nexus...*Joey.*"

Palmer was badgering him, and I didn't know why. Maybe he was trying to goad him into the next round of one-upmanship or something. For whatever reason, Josef Schliemann seemed able to bring out the worst in my husband. I tugged at Palmer's shirt-waist as a plea for him to get a grip.

Schliemann seemed mesmerized by the platform of stone at his feet. He stared at it, wide-eyed; his followers did the same.

"You still haven't answered my question, Joey," Palmer continued.

"Palmer, please," I whispered.

"Now what?" he spat at Schliemann.

"It's enough already," I said.

"Now what?" Schliemann mocked. "Now what?" He looked at me, pointing as if in accusation. "Molly knows, don't you Moll?" He snapped his fingers as if remembering something. "Oh, that's right. You never cared to read *all* of Archambault's journals, did you? Only some, and then you took *my* word as the gospel, didn't you?"

My mouth moved as if to say something clever, but I could think of nothing. I looked at Palmer, but he was fixated on Schliemann. His posture indicated he was about ready to pounce on him to defend my honour should Schliemann go too far.

"That, my dear, was your mistake. *Bias,* my friend. For as long as there has been recorded history, there has been bias. The pen that records history, *makes* history. Yes, I translated Archambault's work, but only the parts I wanted others to know.

"Archambault rallied the natives to build this church, that much you know. You also know that he assimilated with the people he lived with.

"They made him band leader. He ruled over them, amassing wealth which he stored underground, here, in these caverns.

"As the time for him to return home grew near, Archambault's people completed the catacombs. In a final vie for supreme power, he had the sacred altar, the Gateway, transferred to *this* room, had his people record *his* story on these walls. Devised these rings as a testament to his voice—three rings: one representing the sky, the other representing the earth, and the third, in the centre, linking the other two, representing Archambault himself.

"You see, he knew he would have to go home, had visions of what was in store for him. He wrote that it had come to him in a dream; the gods were behind him, you see. One platform here. Hidden. Safe. The other, in his native France. Each imbued with the power of the Nexus, the spiritual centre of the generations, inextricably linked. One here, one in France, and Archambault, the link that would bring the two together. All he had to do was construct the second platform and he would be brought back to this very spot."

"You're talking about a teleportation device. There are plans for something like that in his journals," I told him.

He smiled. "So you *did* read the journals after all."

"As much as my junior high school French would allow." We smiled at each other for a second or two and then I said, "Josef? Um...Archambault...he never returned."

He reached out and caressed the object in front of him. "He was never allowed to finish the device. But the power..." He'd whispered the word "power" as his eyes focussed off into distant space, his lips curled into a thoughtful smile, his eyes gleaming. "The power remains. It is strong. Here. In this room."

"Okay," Palmer began, "I've just about had enough of this shit." He kicked the stone carving; Schliemann started as if he thought Palmer was about to kick him. "It's a rock, okay? There's no power here."

"Josef?" I said as I maneuvered myself between him and my husband; it was a tight squeeze, what with all of the people in the room. Why don't we take a break? I was going to ask, go upstairs and think things through? Josef Schliemann was a good scientist; I've used his books as texts for many of my classes over the years. His writing voice was strong; his ability to persuade powerful. To sell yourself as an expert of the unexplained was one thing, but when you actually began to believe *you* were one of the unexplained— that was something else entirely. My objective at that point was to get Schliemann out of the room and calm him down, gently edge him back toward reality.

As I excused myself across the room, I tripped on a rock sticking up from the soil and fell forward. When I looked up, I noticed the Nexus was...effervescing. Tiny silver bubbles originating from its core floated upward toward the ceiling. As they hit the ceiling, they branched out, like a clinging vine. Steam permeated from the ground around the circumference of the circle.

"Behold!" Schliemann bellowed once more, capitalizing on the special effects, manipulating the situation to his advantage. "The Nexus!" And he stepped onto the centre of the platform, and disappeared, cloaked by the tendrils of smoke growing ever fatter and taller as Jack's beanstalk. When it seemed as though the mist would swallow up every person and object in the room, it started to thin. When it turned from opaque to gauzy, I took a quick head count—Schliemann was gone!

"Where is he?" I asked. "Where's Schliemann?"

People milled about like dazed sheep, gazing upon each other's faces, taking stock.

"Son of a bitch!" I said, standing too quickly, almost losing my balance in the process. Roughly, I pushed through the wad of people blocking the cavern door until I was more or less expectorated into the rough, inadequately lit corridor; Schliemann was nowhere to be seen.

I looked back into the Chamber of the Nexus—Schliemann's followers had dropped to their knees, every one of them without fail, their collective gaze locked on the hunk of rock in the middle of the room.

"Clear the room," I commanded. "Now. Everyone out."

No one moved, neither my students nor Schliemann's followers.

"Now! Let's go!" I yelled, my voice echoing bluntly in the small, damp chamber.

A few of the kneeling fools stood and wandered aimlessly toward me, while others had to be helped to their feet and guided out of the room by my students. As they left, I worked my way back to the Nexus.

"Molly," Palmer said, pleadingly, "calm down."

"He tampered with my site, Palmer."

"*If* the site's authentic, you mean."

I knew that Schliemann's magical ascent in a puff of smoke had been faked, but this was the first time I'd ever considered the entire site might have been hoaxed. I could feel my jaw tighten, my cheeks redden; my teeth grind together.

Palmer rested his hand on my shoulder and shook his head. "This is what Joey does, Moll," he apologized. "He's like a black hole, sucking up all of the attention within a ten-mile radius anywhere he goes in the world."

Up until then, I'd been staring at the Nexus, could not remove my eyes from it, my mind racing, trying to figure out how he'd done it. There had been no evidence the site had been tampered with as we'd dug—the soil had been evenly and tightly compacted throughout. I'd have known if someone had planted the stone there and set us up; I'd have known.

"Molly?" Palmer said. He squeezed my arm gently. "It's over, Moll. It's over."

In the end, it was the way he looked at me that got me. The way he smiled at me, with a closed mouth and wide eyes that got me going. I didn't think I could live the rest of my life fielding condolences and looks of pity like the one I saw on my husband's face at that very moment. I couldn't bear it. I had to find out how Schliemann had done it.

"I want to know how he did it," I said deliberately, surprised at how calm my voice sounded.

"Molly," Palmer chimed.

"No. I won't be made a fool of." I closed my eyes and took a deep breath in an effort to remain calm, counting to ten before continuing. "He tampered with my site, Palmer. I want to know what he did."

He nodded, much to my surprise.

Without so much as another word spoken between us, we assumed mirror positions, squatting at opposite ends of the Nexus. We struggled trying to lift it without success until others joined us, unsolicited. Together, we raised the stone ring and propped it against the far wall of the chamber. Palmer grabbed his trowel and began to dig further. I stood to search for my own trowel and follow suit, but something caught my eye. On the wall, just above where the Nexus was positioned, were glyphs I hadn't noticed before. I hadn't noticed them before because they weren't there to notice, I'm sure of that.

Beside the drawing of Archambault being carted off in chains were three further tableaux. The first depicted a man dressed in black, wearing the symbol of the Fellowship, those three, interconnected rings, on his chest. He stood upon what was unmistakably the Nexus, arms raised to the heavens. The next drawing showed the same figure encircled by a series of animal skin-clad people, kneeling before him in reverence. The final drawing seemed to be a copy of the second, the figure at the centre the only difference. In the last scene, it was a man wearing animal skins that stood on the Nexus as he was given glory by the people.

"Molly," Palmer called. I turned my head in the direction of his voice. "You need to see this."

I grabbed my trowel and kneeled, facing him on the floor. He was on his knees which were nearly hidden by a thick blanket of dirt, using a small whisk broom to further clear what he'd found.

As he swept, a white, spherical globe came into view. He swept some more and I could make out the high dome of a forehead, and then skeletal eye and nose sockets. I grabbed a whisk and helped him further clear the skeleton: lower jaw, cervical vertebrae, and clavicle. I turned to get the camera. When I looked back, I could hardly believe what I saw.

Around the neck of the skeleton was a diamond-cut gold chain. On the chain was a small pendant: three interlocked rings that had come to symbolize Josef Schliemann's organization. I picked the pendant up in my hand, polishing it between my fingers and thumb.

"He who rules the Nexus rules the world, right?" Palmer said.

I looked from the pendant to the skeleton and then to my husband. "'There are more things in heaven and earth than modern man will ever know or understand'," I said, hearing my voice as though from a million miles away.

"What's that?" Palmer asked.

"Huh? Oh, nothing. Just something Schliemann once told me."

I turned the pendant over in my hand, rubbing the back of it to remove the small particles of dirt left sticking to the metal. As I rubbed, I noticed there was an engraving on the back of the pendant. I brought the find to Palmer's attention. He blinked, as speechless as was I.

On the back of the pendant, etched in neat script, were two small initials: J.S.

HOT OFF THE PRESSES!

THE NEW RECRUIT

"You know that feeling when you're totally fangirling a new YA and you want more, more, more? When you discover a new author and you just can't get enough? That's how I feel after reading Elise Abram...*The New Recruit* is a plot-driven emotional rollercoaster."

—Maria Samurin, author

Rescuing food from the dumpster to feed the hungry, spending the weekend picking up garbage in a park, and attending peaceful protests all seem like great ways to make the world a better place but...

What if it's not enough?

When sixteen-year-old Judith meets Cain, she has no idea what she's getting herself into. Cain is the most beautiful human being Judith has ever seen, but he hides a dangerous secret. When Jo-Jo, Cain's surrogate father, offers her a job, she accepts, unaware she's been recruited as a pawn in Jo-Jo's ecoterrorist plot.

Will Judith find a way out before it's too late?
Does she have a choice?

In a time when jobs are scarce, politics are unstable, and the future is uncertain, all of us are vulnerable, willing to blindly follow a charismatic leader in exchange for the promise of a stable world view.

I WAS, AM, WILL BE ALICE

For readers of TIME TRAVELER'S WIFE and ALICE IN WONDERLAND

Winner of the 2015 A Woman's Write Competition for Fiction!

When Alice Carroll is in grade three she narrowly escapes losing her life in a school shooting. All she remembers is the woman comforting her in the moments before the gunshot, and that one second she was there, the next she wasn't.

It's bad enough coming to terms with surviving while others, including her favourite teacher, didn't, let alone dealing with the fact she might wink out of existence at any time.

Alice spends the next few years seeing specialists about her Post Traumatic Stress as a result of VD—Voldemort Day—but it's not until she has a nightmare about The Day That Shall Not Be Mentioned, disappears from her bed, is found by police, and taken home to meet her four-year-old self that she realizes she's been time travelling.

Alice is unsure if her getting unstuck in time should be considered an ability or a liability, until she disappears right in front of her high school at dismissal time, the busiest time of day. Worried that someone may find out about her problem before long, Alice enlists her best friend (and maybe boyfriend), Pete, to help her try to control her shifting through time with limited success. She's just about ready to give up when the shooter is caught. Alice resolves to take control of her time travelling in order to go back to That Day, stop the shooting, and figure out the identity of the stranger who'd shielded Alice's body with her own.

IF YOU LIKED "ALIENS' WALTZ" AND "THE NEXUS"...

THE FURTHER ADVENTURES OF

MOLLY, PALMER, AND SCHLIEMANN IN

PHASE SHIFT

If you knew the world were about to end, what would you do?

If you found the key to another Earth, would you use it?

When archaeologist Molly McBride finds the key to a doppelganger Earth she is swept into a world of conspiracy that could end in the death of not one, but two planets.

Will Molly be able to prevent the impending cataclysm?

MORE ABOUT MOLLY AND PALMER

THROWAWAY CHILD

The skeleton of a young girl is found beneath the cement basement floor in an abandoned Victorian in Toronto. On duty is Detective Constable Michael Crestwood who contacts forensic anthropologist Dr. Palmer Richardson to assist in the investigation. What they uncover is the story of a six year old Cree girl, stolen from her family, warehoused in a government run facility and then forgotten.

In a story with ties to current headlines, THROWAWAY CHILD explores the injustice experienced by two girls imprisoned in a mid-twentieth century residential school and the tragic fallout ensuing as a result of one girl's need to find a home.

THE MUMMY WORE COMBAT BOOTS

When called to investigate an uncatalogued sarcophagus found in storage at the Royal Ontario Museum, forensic anthropologist Palmer Richardson has his work cut out for him. When the mummy inside proves to be that of a teenage boy, Palmer joins Detective Constable Michael Crestwood of the Metropolitan Toronto Police. in an investigation delving into the world of online gaming where losing health points in a skirmish could have serious implications for a player's life in the real world.

Inspired by real-life headlines, THE MUMMY WORE COMBAT BOOTS highlights the growing divide between children who live their lives immersed in a digital culture and the adults tasked with raising them who live in the real world.

www.ingramcontent.com/pod-product-compliance
Lightning Source LLC
Chambersburg PA
CBHW051305170626
46809CB00004B/1773